Christie Moore has played bass in a rock band for many years and worked in many aspects of the music industry. She has self-published three books but, being a lover of science fiction and history, it is no surprise that a historical novel would soon appear and this is her second. Inspired by a visit to a re-enactment and watching two female knights fight, Lady Leah was soon hatched into an idea.

LADY LEAH OF LYGETON

Christie Moore

LADY LEAH OF LYGETON

Vanguard Press

VANGUARD PAPERBACK

© Copyright 2018
Christie Moore

A CIP catalogue record for this title is
available from the British Library.

ISBN 978 1 784654 05 4

Vanguard Press is an imprint of
Pegasus Elliot MacKenzie Publishers Ltd.
www.pegasuspublishers.com

First published in 2018

Vanguard Press
Sheraton House Castle Park
Cambridge England

Printed and bound in Great Britain

Dedication

My Auntie Brenda, for reading through my story.

My friend Leah for the inspiration for the story.

The two unknown lady knights I saw years ago at a re-enactment that gave me the initial idea for the story.

During the twelfth to fourteenth centuries were the times of knights and chivalry. Knights were always men but history has shown that indeed some women became knights; these women were frowned upon. This is the story of one of those women.

Chapter 1

The Joust

The year is 1332. The place is England and experiencing a period of peace, the Scottish were defeated at the Battle of Dupplin Moor; however it was nothing to do with the king but a bunch of his nobles decided to fight the Scots who then put their own Scottish king in place. The Scots chased this new king out of Scotland who then ran back to the king of England for protection. The Scots were now in negotiations with the French to form an alliance which could mean trouble ahead for England. The young King Edward III of England is trying to forget all that and is hosting a series of jousting tournaments across the country, the time is the end of August and it is a typical English summer of overcast cloud with the forever potential threat of rain. Edward is only twenty years old but has the manner of someone much older; he has been king now for four years. This particular joust is at Dunstable, the jousting ground being west of Watling Street and south of the Icknield Way. Off in the distance to the east can be seen the huge church of Saint Mary's and the Augustinian priory, whilst in the west are the rolling hills of the Downs. The jousting ring has been used for many years now, having the odd touch-up to keep it in order. King Edward and his queenly wife Philippa are hosting this year's jousting tournament which should be interesting as there are new faces on the scene. Surrounding the royal couple are dignitaries from the local area including the bishops of both Dunstable and nearby Lygeton. War is always on the horizon but for now nobody cares, they just want to have a good time. The food sellers walk around with their wares:

"Get your gyngerbrede!"

"Get your marzipan tart, prince bisket!"

"Get your Spanish pastries. Try out your sweet tooth!"

The food sellers do a roaring trade owing much to the introduction of sugar in all things sweet, giving people a buzz and they want more. There are displays of falconry which much impresses the king, and jesters, musicians as well as many other kinds of acts. It was as much a day out for peasant families as it was for anybody else. King Edward turns to his wife, "I think my dear; this will be the best games ever."

"Why so?" she asks.

"I don't know, I just want to forget the whole incident of Dupplin Moor."

"More like you're just gearing up for another war, you men do like a good punch-up"

"Never mind that, I have heard there is a special star of a knight competing today."

"Oh goody, I do hope he's handsome." The queen claps her hands together.

"Yes well, I want to know who he is."

"So you can stick him in your army for your next war?"

The apprentice knights are the first to come out of their tents one by one in their chain-mail armour whilst the ladies blush. They're introduced by Lord Zuckerman:

"Sir Glenn of Hertfordshire."

Sir Glenn steps out looking resplendent.

"Sir Thomas of London."

Another fine-looking knight.

"Sir Gawain of Liverpool."

After every knight announced the crowd get louder.

"Sir Edward of Reading."

Much louder.

"Sir Vincent of Canterbury."

The peasants have seen nothing like this before.

"Sir Alexander of London."

The knights just keep coming.

"Sir Leon of Leeds."

And coming.

"And last year's winner, Sir James of Ireland."

The crowd go wild as the line of knights comes out. These are newish knights, although they were all in the joust competition last year they have had no battle experience and, since then, they still have no battle experience. These new knights are hoping that the king will notice them and ask if they can join his army or at least be granted some lands of their own. They are pleased to be here and play up to the crowd's excitement but fail to see the next knight coming out of his tent, who stands with his hands on his hips. Whereas all the other knights are wearing chain mail with an outer linen covering, this next knight is wearing a breastplate made of tempered iron over his chain mail, where the plate is hammered over a hot stove and some charcoal is added to create a hardened metal that does not shatter when struck. This is the newest technology to arrive in England from Europe and the knight is well off enough to purchase this latest advance in body armour. The knight is very tall and handsome, but has an air of arrogance about him.

"Sir Richard of Bedford!" announces Lord Zuckerman.

The confident knight strides forward and pushes aside Sir James.

"Make way for the real knight, sonny."

The crowd cheer for Sir Richard while he stands posing and looking really smug with himself; people in the crowd talk amongst themselves.

"Look, he has the latest body armour."

The ladies blush.

"Oh, he looks so handsome."

"I think he is looking at me!"

As Sir Richard walks off, the next knight stumbles out and is having trouble getting his helmet off. It seems to be stuck fast; the knight pushes and pulls causing the huge pink feather attached to the top of the helmet to sway backwards and forwards. This knight also has full plate chest armour, but in addition has plate metal covering the forearms and lower legs over the top of his chain mail. Lord Zuckerman looks at the list in disbelief and says "this can't be right."

The knight replies in a mumbled voice, "Just say it.

Lord Zuckerman puts down the list and just stares at the knight, who continues to struggle with the tight helmet.

The knights move out to their horses and wait for their turn. The king stands up holding a hankerchief with an outstretched arm to an anticipating crowd. He turns to the queen.

My dear, prepare yourself for the most exciting games ever."

She giggles and the king announces loudly. "Let the games begin."

He then releases the hankerchief which drops slowly to the ground, the royal trumpeters sound their trumpets and the games are under way. The first two knights to fight are Sir James and Sir Leon, both astride their fine horses. After the flag is raised in the centre of the jousting ring, the horses charge at each other on either side of the cloth barrier or tilt. Sir James makes contact with his opponent, his lance splinters into a thousand pieces and Sir Leon is knocked clean off his horse and lands with a thud on the ground. The crowd go wild. Sir Leon lifts up his visor to be confronted with a stubby finger pointing at him.

"You're fired," says Lord Zuckerman.

Sir Leon is carried off on a litter. Then Sir Richard faces Sir Thomas, they charge and Sir Thomas is knocked off. Again, while he is lying on the floor, he sees Lord Zuckerman pointing at him:

"You're fired."

He is carried off. Next to be knocked off by Sir Richard is Sir Alexander.

"You're fired."

Then Sir Edward.

"You're fired."

Next up is Sir Gawain who faces up to the knight with no name who is astride a brilliant white horse. There is a hush in the crowd. The queen sits forward on her seat. The flag is raised. The two charge at each other, there is an almighty crash and Sir Gawain's lance is splintered as he falls to the floor. Gawain gets up clumsily and says, "Yes I know. I'm fired.""

Although Gawain is standing he is still carried off on a litter.

"Let me go, I'm all right he shouts as he is carried off.

"Who is this knight?" asks the queen to her husband.

"I know not, my dear," he replies.

Sir Glenn and Sir Vincent are next, they clash and Sir Vincent is fired but Sir Glenn is dispensed with by Sir Richard.

"You're fired."

Glenn is carried off. Sir James is knocked off by the knight with no name and falls to the ground clumsily.

"You're fired."

***

Sir James feels unwell after being clobbered so heavily; he lifts his head up and sees his lower leg sticking straight up into the air.

"My leg!" he wails. "It's broken."

The two stretcher bearers turn up to carry James off to the hospital, which is on the other side of Watling Street attached to the priory at Saint Mary's Church. On entry into the hospital he is told to confess and then pray for his sins by the bishop.

"I don't want to pray!" he shouts, "I just want me leg fixed."

"Come now young man, prayer to God is the only sure way to heal yourself; illness is just your sins collecting up over the years. Now what do you want to confess?"

James grimaces from the pain of the broken leg.

"I was the winner of last year's tournament but I lost this year," he says as quickly as he can get his words out.

"That will do," said the bishop and he made the sign of the cross with his hand. All the while Sir James could hear a choir singing in the background.

James is placed on a bed in a large dormitory where a little sunlight streams through open windows up top. He is stripped of his armour by three nuns; they pull off the chain mail and let it drop to the floor while the knight lifts his head and can see his bare leg still sticking up in the air. In the bed next to him is Antwon the mad monk.

"I'll have some ham, a flagon of mead and a piece of that cheese over there."

The head nun of the three turns and says to the monk, "Antwon, stop messing about and get back to your duties."

"The food's better in here than we get in the priory," replies Antwon.

He reluctantly gets up and saunters off. During that few moments, Sir James looks around him and he sees the other apprentice knights eating, Sir Glenn turns to James and says, "This is better food than I can afford at home."

With the renegade mad monk dealt with, the three nuns turn their attention once again to Sir James just as another monk turns up, obviously someone important as he has an air of importance about him.

"Now," says the monk, let's have a look and see what the problem is."

"My leg's broken," replies Sir James.

"Don't interrupt young man," snaps the monk. "I am the doctor here."

He turns to the younger nun, "Nurse, get the leeches."

"What? It's my leg that's broken, I don't have an illness," James protests again as a bucket is brought out from some unknown place.

"I don't need those; my leg needs to be fixed."

The three nuns ignore the protests of the young knight and start attaching leeches to his bare legs.

"Come on, lift up your vest," says the head nun.

James complies but as soon as any bare skin is revealed the nuns attach leeches to his stomach and chest.

"When are you going to fix my leg?"

Two of the nuns quickly run off to attend to another patient while the leeches gorge themselves on James's blood.

"The bone-setter will be with you soon," says the doctor monk, who then turns and walks away.

"Antwon! Leave that food alone," cries the head nun pointing to the mad monk and she too leaves Sir James alone. Sir James looks despairingly down at the now fat leeches heaving up and down on his gorged blood while his lower leg still points upwards.

All the knights have been dispensed with and the last two contestants face each other: Sir Richard and the knight with no name. Tension builds up as the two knights square each other up, their lances are held upright. The crowd are quiet with anticipation as they first look at Sir Richard astride his coal black horse with his shield showing the sign of the weasel, then they all turn their heads to the knight with no name astride the brilliant white horse and whose shield bears a pair of lions, one above the other. Who will the crowd go for? The handsome knight whose face they have seen? Or maybe the knight with no name who might be handsome, but people can't tell; this knight might be ugly for all they know. But the crowd love the expectancy. The trumpeter sounds a note, the flag is raised on the jousting field and Sir Richard gets his horse galloping whilst the knight with no name rears up on the white horse: the two knights charge. Drum, drum, drum go the horse's hooves on the ground as the two knights gallop towards each other at high speed, the crowd gasp in apprehension not knowing who they want to win. The knights lower their lances which both splinter, but both contestants stay in their saddles, their lances are quickly replaced and they charge again. The air of excitement is too much for some of the ladies who faint, but Sir Richard is knocked off straightaway, much to the disbelief of the crowd.

"Who is this knight?" murmurs someone.

The new knight dismounts and draws a sword while Sir Richard gets up, also drawing his sword. The two weapons clash with a mighty noise, but Richard is quick to throw another strike which is deflected by the knight with no name. He swings and makes contact with Richard's breastplate, but the sword just bounces off.

The king turns to his wife and says, "I didn't think they continued with sword fighting, that's not in the rules. Still, I'm not complaining. They can carry on if they like, makes it more interesting."

Eventually Sir Richard is beaten to the ground with a hefty swipe to his helmet. The crowd go quiet. Sir Richard is dazed but manages to get his helmet off. Everything is blurred but he manages to make out the stubby finger that is inches from his face.

"YOU'RE FIRED"

Two men grab Sir Richard by the arms but he shouts, "You cheated!"

"Come now Sir Richard," says Lord Zuckerman. "You were beaten fair and square."

The new knight tries to get the tight helmet off but it's still stuck, the large pink feather still waving around. There is still no noise until the knight gives up with the helmet and raises both hands, and then the crowd go wild while Sir Richard is dragged off.

The knight with no name is presented to the king and queen, albeit he is still having trouble with getting the helmet off.

"What is your name sir knight?" asks the queen.

Just then a woman runs up to the knight holding an iron bar. She is a tall woman and is well built, making it obvious to those around her that she has done some hard work in her life. She is wearing a long green leather dress with her hair braided. She inserts the iron bar underneath the knight's helmet.

"Who are you?" asks the king.

The woman withdraws the iron bar and turns to the king

"I'm Christine," she says.

"But what are you doing here?" the king continues with his questioning.

"Oh, I'm the squire, your majesty."

"What! But you're a woman!"

"Yes, well I was the last time I looked."

The king started to get a bit agitated by now.

"This is no laughing matter. Squires are never women."

Christine puts the iron bar back into the helmet of the still struggling knight.

"Except me of course."

The queen interjects.

"Look, just let him lift his visor up" the queens says, as she offers her hand.

"Are you sure?" says Christine as she brings the iron bar down to the side of her leg. "I mean it wouldn't be right to…"

"Yes I'm sure!" snaps the queen still holding her hand out.

Christine guides the knight over and lifts up the visor; all that can be seen is the knight's lips. The queen holds her hand up to the knight's face.

"Huh?" mumbles the knight.

"Just kiss her hand and let's get out of here," says Christine quietly to the knight.

"I told you not to make my helmet so small, didn't I?" mumbles the knight to Christine.

The queen has her hand kissed then withdraws and sits down, while Christine resumes trying to get the helmet off the knight. She prises a bit more but the helmet gets stuck on the knight's nose.

"Ow, my nose!" the knight cries.

Suddenly the helmet breaks free and drops to the floor, long blonde hair tumbles out and around the shoulders of the knight. The queen stands up horrified.

"A woman?" she screams.

"Yes your majesty," says the knight. "My name is Lady Leah of Lygeton."

"It's pronounced Lieton," says the king, slightly amused.

The queen gets angrier. "I don't care how it's pronounced; you can't have a woman knight!"

"Ooh now, now my dear, you're not upset that your hand was kissed by a..." the king stifles a laugh ... "a woman?"

Lady Leah and Christine just stand there while the king and queen have a married tiff.

"You've got to banish her!" cries the queen.

"Bit harsh innit?" says Lady Leah.

"We can't banish her for being a woman," replies the king "I have to consult parliament first."

"Yes you can," says the queen getter louder. "YOU'RE THE KING!"

"Well yes, I suppose I can banish anybody I like."

"Then do it!" cries the queen pointing to Lady Leah.

"All right then, you're banished from my kingdom for five years," says the king to Lady Leah.

Leah's face drops. Christine drops her iron bar. Sir Richard sidles up to the pair and declares, "Does that make me the winner then?"

"Yes," says the queen positively and she offers her hand for Sir Richard to kiss, which he does with relish and then turns slyly to Lady Leah and gives one of his arrogant grins.

"What about people's rights as written in the Magna Carta?" protests Leah.

"That applies to men only, a woman is a man's property" replies the king. "Who is your husband?"

"I am unmarried."

"Do you have a father?"

"No he died fighting in Ireland."

"Then you have no rights, now you may leave."

Christine hands over to Leah some parchments from her shoulder bag. "My lady, your documents."

"Yes," says Leah, taking the parchment and handing them to the king. My heraldic documents."

The king takes the parchments and studies them.

"Oh, your father was Sir Bertram?"

"Yes, your majesty," replies Leah.

"Your family goes back quite a way, I see."

The king hands the documents back to Leah who then hands them to Christine, who then puts them away in her small bag.

"Your documents are in order but it makes no difference. You are a woman and therefore you forfeit your right to win this tournament."

Lady Leah picks up her helmet; she and Christine mope off, Leah's armour chinking as she walks. Lord Zuckerman declares loudly, "You're a lightweight, you're FIRED."

Sir Richard is well pleased with himself and grins like a Cheshire cat.

"I am the best knight ever!" he shouts as he does a little dance.

Leah mounts her horse and rides off leaving Christine to follow with the rest of the knightly gear in her arms, whilst the crowd turn their attentions to partying; the court musicians start playing their instruments. But Richard hasn't finished yet, he walks up to the crowd behind the barriers and raises his arms. The crowd cheer their excitement.

"I am the winner!" declares Sir Richard, urging the crowd to cheer some more.

Chapter 2

The Exile

Lady Leah sits in her castle in Leagrave Marshes just north of Lygeton, not a huge castle but it does have a surrounding wall and a moat. It is two storeys high and square, with turrets on each corner. Since it is so small it doesn't have many staff. Surrounding the castle is marshy ground while the Icknield Way runs close by with many travellers travelling by. Near the castle is a large circular mound which at the centre is the source of the River Lea. Many have said this is a mystical and ancient place which is why the castle was built there in the first place. Christine gathers together important stuff whilst her Lady Leah sits at a table with her elbow on the table and her chin resting on her hand; she just sits and contemplates. Leah realises that by the time she comes back the castle will be in someone else's hands or even left to ruin, this castle that was her father's but passed on to his only heir, Leah. Over there in the corner is her father's chain mail armour, the same armour he fought with during the Despenser Wars in 1322. The same armour he died in fighting at the Battle of Fiodh-an-Átha against Ualgarg O'Rourke, the King of Bréifne. That was two years ago. The armour glistens in the light thanks to Christine polishing it every day. That wasn't one of her duties but she did it anyway as she didn't like the idea of it going brown with rust. The family banner hung proudly in the main hall showing its two lions one above the other; she was very sad but banishment was to be taken seriously and so she came out of her contemplation to prepare to leave.

Sir Richard is in his mother's room conversing with her.

"I'm the winner of this year's joust," he declares happily whilst doing a little dance. He repeated himself again, "I'm the winner of this year's joust."

"It's not made you rich though, has it?" says Mother in a sarcastic tone.

"Eh?" Richard suddenly stops his little dance. "I'm well off."

"Yes, but not filthily fantastically rich, are you?"

"Well no."

"You've disgraced one knight, how about others?"

"I don't understand mother."

"Oh, you silly boy. There are other knights with secrets to expose."

"What do you mean? Give me an example."

"There's Sir Harold, I'm sure his wife and his fiefdom would like to know about his mistress he has on the side."

"All knights have mistresses, Mother."

"Don't declare something like that to your wife now, will you?"

"Me? I don't have a mistress"

"What? Are you not a man?"

"Well... I... er."

"Forget about that, back to Sir Harold."

"Yes, but I don't think many people would take an interest."

"They would if they knew that his mistress was the daughter of the king's cousin. That would be a treasonable offence."

"So I tell everyone, do I?" asks a bewildered Richard.

Mother stands up quickly and walks to the window, turns and says, "No you silly boy, you tell Sir Harold that you know and demand a huge sum of money to keep your mouth shut."

***

Leah knows that now is the time to inform her staff.

"Christine, call the servants together."

Christine goes off into the depths of the castle leaving Leah with her thoughts. She drifts back to when she first saw her father fighting when she was aged just five years old. She watches from the upstairs window while Father trains with his squire. The swords clang together while little Leah watches with fascination. She rushes downstairs holding the hem of her dress up and in a rack is a collection of swords; she stands for a moment, so many swords to choose from. Finally she decides and pulls the smallest sword out by the handle but it is still as long as she is tall. She manages to lift it up in the air but it is too heavy, she totters around uneasily on her feet whilst holding the sword above her head and it comes crashing to the floor just as her father walks in. She declares to him, "I want to be a knight just like you when I grow up," much to the amusement of her father who guffaws loudly in his gruff voice. Leah hears a noise which breaks her out of her reminiscence. It is the first of the servants followed quickly by all the others who gather together in the main hall. Christine has also joined the group, and so Leah stands up.

"My faithful servants," she begins, "I have important news for you."

There is unease amongst them, announcements like this are rarely good news.

"I have been punished by the king and I am to be exiled from this fine country for a term of five years. This means I will not be able to pay your wages. If you wish to leave then I give you permission to find alternative employment."

"Well, we'll pack our things then," mutters Walter Neville as he turns to his wife Beatrice.

"I've worked here for years," mutters Johannes, a well-built, strong man.

"I've worked under your father," declares Carle Ballard, a small weasel-looking man.

Joan just shrugs her shoulders; she doesn't know what she will do as she's an old woman and has no chance of finding another job at her age. The servants break up and head for their bed chambers to pack. Leah sits down rather glumly.

"It's come to this, has it?"

Christine lays a hand on Leah's shoulder.

"You don't have to come with me Christine. I'm the one being banished."

"My Lady," declares Christine, "I am your assistant, I will come with you."

Leah looks up at Christine. "Thank you," she says meekly.

***

"Then there's Sir Roger," says Mother

"Who's Sir Roger?" replies her son.

"You know, that one with the awful moustache and the stupid voice."

Mother stops suddenly and looks at her son; she questions her own son's voice.

"Anyway, I've heard he keeps a bunch of young lads in his castle."

"They're his serfs," says Richard.

"You really are naive; they are a bit finely dressed to be his serfs."

"Maybe they are his knights in training?"

"No you stupid boy, they are his boys, you know, think. He doesn't have girls around his place, just boys."

"Huh? No? Not Sir Roger. He would be very disliked by all if that were the case."

"Precisely. And you pay him a visit and tell him you know about his filthy little habits. Then you demand money to keep your mouth shut, after all, remind him what happened to the king's father"

"Oh yes, the king's father, he had a hot poker up the bum."

Richard would have laughed at his own remark but couldn't due to a swift hand round the back of his head.

"Don't be so vulgar," Mother says angrily.

***

Bishop Gilbert has shown up and is shown in by Christine.

"My Lady," he starts in his strong Irish accent, but is unable to continue.

"I know," says Leah, "but I have to go."

"I did warn you, you know, but you continued with this foolhardy action. I knew your father and I don't think he would have approved."

"I knew my father better and I say he would have approved."

"Yes but a woman meddling in men's affairs, it's just not right."

"Why not?"

"Because women are the property of their husbands or fathers and as you have neither... "

"Yes, as has been pointed out to me," remarks Leah glumly.

"You only kept your father's property because I granted you rights to own them."

"Yes, and I will be eternally grateful to you for that."

"You know your mother tried to take possession of your lands."

"My mother?" remarks Leah. "You knew her?"

"I never met her, she communicated through letters. But your father's will was explicit. You were to inherit his lands. "He was determined for a long time to see you have his property."

"Yes thank you"

Leah is still sitting while Gilbert looks down on her from his standing position.

"Well, whatever you do I will pray to God to see you safe in your endeavours."

Leah looks up to Gilbert's face.

"Thank you Bishop."

"I say," says the bishop diverting his attention elsewhere, "those bottles of wine over there, you don't need them now, do you?"

Leah looks up. "No, take them"

"It's for Mass."

Gilbert gathers six bottles and manages to hold them all by having some between his arms and body.

"Just think of it as your tithe."

Gilbert turns and walks towards the door but stops and looks back towards Leah.

"Good luck Lady Leah and I will see you in five years' time."

***

"And then..." continues Mother, "with Lady Leah out of the way for a while Lygeton has no knight to defend it."

"I could take Matilda shopping there," says Richard with his back to his mother, fist on hip and other hand stroking his chin. Suddenly Richard gets a whack round the back of his head again with Mother's hand.

"You dim boy, no you take a group of men and you raid the place. You don't want to give that town any money; you take what they have for yourself."

"Brilliant mother, you're a genius." Richard rubs the back of his head.

"A cockerel is a genius compared to you."

"Huh?" says Richard.

"We're going to travel," Leah said to Christine.

"Travel, where to m'lady?"

"Oh, I don't know, maybe the Middle East or even Africa."

Christine stood there with a bunch of clothing across her arms with a thoughtful look on her face.

"I'd like to see Europe, I've heard the Kingdom of Hungary is interesting, then there's France..."

"Too much garlic," interrupted Leah.

"Or the Holy Roman Empire of Germany, or even Byzantium."

The pair sat quietly for a moment, then Leah speaks up:

"We could see the Pope in Rome."

"Er, m'lady, the Pope's in Avignon."

"Where's Avignon?"

"South of France."

"What? When did he move? Why did no one tell me?"

Lady Leah stood up and took a few steps forward and pursed her lips.

"I'll have to sleep on it."

Leah turns towards Christine.

"We leave in the morning," and with that she disappears off up to her chamber.

Christine doesn't know what to do; she puts down the pile of clothing on the table, gets out a cloth and starts polishing the chain-mail armour in the corner.

***

Richard has gone downstairs to the main hall where his wife is sitting with her ladies-in-waiting, who are sewing tapestries.

"Matilda my darling," says Richard, "we are going to be rich."

"That's nice dear. How are you going to do that?"

Richard stands with his back to his wife with his fists on his hips, the ladies-in-waiting not stopping the tempo of their sewing at all.

"With great ingenuity, my dear."

"Oh yes, are you going to tell me more"

"No" says Richard, "I need to have something to eat, I will ask the kitchen staff to prepare me something to eat, I'm famished."

"It is a bit late in the evening," replies his wife.

"Nonetheless, I will have something to eat. I am after all the greatest knight in all of England and this greatness needs a large intake of food to sustain it."

He is still standing with his fists on his hips, hoping all the women behind him are impressed with him.

In the morning Richard's household is having breakfast including his wife and his mother, while Carle Ballard has turned up at the door of Bedford Castle.

"I can be of service to you, Sir Richard," he says standing in the main hall in front of a disinterested Sir Richard.

"How so, serf?" says Richard, not breaking his rhythm of eating.

"I was previously in the service of Sir Bertram of Lygeton."

"Ah, Lady Leah's father." Now Richard is interested and he sits up.

"Yes my lord. But she is an abomination. You can't have a woman knight, can you sir?"

"Certainly not. But she is leaving the country, is she not?"

"Yes Sir, this morning she leaves but as you can see I am without a job."

Richard's mother leans over.

"Richard my dear," she says into his ear.

"Yes Mother?" he replies.

"You could get rid of that squire of yours, what's his name?"

"Roger."

"Yes, I don't like him, he's weird."

"But I need a squire Mother."

"There is your squire standing in front of you."

"That's an ex-servant of Lady Leah."

"Oh Richard, are you sure you're my son?"

"Huh?" Richard turns to look at his mother fully.

"Listen my boy, he's the perfect squire. He has inside information."

"On what?"

"On Lady Leah."

Richard's brain suddenly gets what his mother is on about and he turns to Ballard.

"Sir, I wish to offer you the job as my squire."

"Sir?" Ballard looks up with a baffled look on his face.

"You heard. My squire, with immediate effect."

In the far corner sits Roger but he stands up, slowly.

"But Sire, I am your squire." he says feebly.

"Not any more you're not. Now leave" Richard holds up a pointing arm.

Roger shuffles uneasily towards the door, but turns to face Richard.

"I have been with your family for years, Sire," he says.

Richard just continues pointing without even looking at Roger, who turns towards the door again but stops and turns back.

"I served under your father."

"OUT!" demands Richard and Roger is out of the room, and Sir Richard's life.

"Now my squire" says Richard, as he addresses Ballard, "take your rightful place."

"Thank you sire," says Ballard. "I will be at your side for always, whatever." Ballard runs off to sit where Roger was sitting. He sits down, admiring around from the new spot he has been given.

Richard sits down only to be scolded by his mother.

"That went well," she says quietly in Richard's ear.

"What do you mean?" asks her son.

"Well, you could have had a bit more tact. Firing Roger like that in front of everybody"

"But you said you didn't like him"

***

Christine has been up for an hour and is packing; she has clothes draped across her arms when Leah walks in.

"I've decided, I want to go somewhere that has unrest. I could do with some battle experience."

Christine drops the clothes.

"M'Lady? But that's dangerous."

"No," says Leah walking off, "my mind's made up, get the travelling gear together and get Joust-a-Lot ready."

"Have I got to carry the stuff again? Can't I have my own horse?" asks Christine.

"No, we can't afford it. You'll just have to carry everything. You're a big girl, you can manage it."

Christine breathes a heavy sigh but Leah's mind is made up.

"Let's go forth and explore."

She pulls her sword out of its sheath and raises it in the air.

"To fame and glory."

Christine just gulps.

***

Matilda is looking for her husband. Breakfast was finished an hour ago but now she wants to talk to her husband. She finds him in the courtyard of the castle standing and watching his serfs load up the horse. Next to him is his mother talking to him, mother notices Matilda coming and quickly walks off.

"Where are you going husband dear?" Matilda asks Richard.

"Going shopping my darling."

"Shopping, where?"

"We're going to Lygeton. I will bring you back something nice."

He kisses her on the cheek and mounts his horse, he turns towards his serfs.

"Men, follow me to Lygeton."

He trots his horse out of the castle courtyard slowly with his grumbling men following behind; it's a long walk to Lygeton from Bedford. Richard turns to wave to his wife who she herself waves back. She watches as Richard on his horse and his nine faithful men follow behind. She watches as they walk off into the distance.

Several hours later Leah has packed (or rather her faithful friend has packed for her) and slung across the back of her white horse. Christine, with her huge backpack slung on her shoulders full of armour and weapons, prepares to follow behind her lady. Leah mounts her horse but pauses to survey the castle; it is now empty of all people and feels eerily quiet. Leah had lived here all her life and now has to leave; this has to be the saddest moment in her life after the death of her father. She turns the horse to leave the castle with Christine following behind, a heavy heart in both women's chests. As they leave the castle, they follow the Icknield Way towards Dunstable, and neither look back. Neither does either see the hordes of figures and horse with rider in the distance appearing over the far end of the circular mound and making their way towards the castle.

Fare thee well, Lygeton.

Chapter 3

The Return

It is 1337 and not much has happened in England for the last five years. There has been relative peace with only one war, that with Scotland at the battle of Halidon Hill. There has been peace between England and France until recently when a few events have turned two friends into rival kings, and with France being an ally of Scotland there may be trouble ahead for England. As for Lady Leah her exile is almost up. She and her squire Christine have been travelling for many weeks now, visiting places on the way and now they have reached Carcassonne in the south of France, they can see the walled city high up on the hill off in the distance. Lady Leah is riding her white horse Joust-a-lot but now she is wearing full armour except for her helmet, which is strapped to the back of her horse. Leah has made some money on her travels.

"This is a fine suit of armour you have made for me, Christine," says Leah proudly.

"Well, I just followed what the Italians were doing; it's the latest you know. Chain mail will be obsolete soon."

The armour glimmers in the sun and Leah looks resplendent in it with her long golden hair flowing down her back. Christine follows on her own horse, a ragged tough old beast which looked as though it could do with a good brushing.

"I'm glad you got me this horse, m'lady."

"Yes, but poor thing must be overloaded with all those mementos you've collected from all those countries."

"Well, I needed memories." Christine pulls out an object from her front bag. "I mean look at this painting of Rome. It looks a right state, no wonder the popes left it."

Christine gees on her horse to get slightly in front of Leah and holds up the small painting to encourage Leah to look at it. However, all Leah was concerned about was that her squire was slightly in front of her and made a motion with her hand to indicate to Christine to move back a bit, and then gee'd up her horse to be in front. Leah slightly turns to Christine, "And why did you have to name her Swiftflight?"

"I like the name."

"Yes, but it's more of a pony than a horse. I should imagine I could run faster than that raggedy old thing, whilst wearing my armour too."

Christine leaned forward and spoke into the horse's ear:

"Don't listen to her Swiftflight, she doesn't mean it."

"And what was that thing we saw in Rome?" asks Leah.

"What thing?" replies Christine.

"That thing that made a loud noise with lots of smoke."

"I believe they called that a cannon. It fires a projectile at high speed. I have heard it can penetrate even armour."

"Where's the honour in that? It'll never catch on you know."

Leah sees the city of Carcassonne in the distance and points to it.

"That big building up there, what is it?" she asks.

"I believe that is the city's cathedral."

Christine pulls out a wooden tube from her pouch which has a glass lens attached to each end.

"What's that?" asks Leah.

Christine has the device to her eye and is looking through it.

"It's my new invention," she declares. "It magnifies distant objects. I can see the cathedral more clearly now."

"Let me see" demands Leah holding out a gloved open hand.

Christine hands the contraption to Leah, who looks through the opposite end. The images off in the distance appear smaller, and the city of Carcassonne looks even further away now.

"It's rubbish," Leah says and tosses the invention into the grass.

"That's going to be very useful you know," wails Christine who stops her horse.

"Come on," demands Leah spurring Christine back into motion, "it will never catch on."

A bark is heard behind them; a terrier is following a short distance behind.

"Where did that hound come from?" asks Leah.

"Somewhere in Naples, I think," replies Christine, "it just keeps following us."

"That's because you keep feeding it."

"I like him, he's cute. I'd like to keep him."

"Well you can't."

"What's wrong with Holdfast?"

"Holdfast? Another silly name you've picked?"

Christine turns slightly on her horse.

"Don't worry Holdfast, my lady didn't mean it."

Leah continues her insults. "It wouldn't be any good for hunting and it needs a good brushing. Look at it, its fur is all sticking up. An untidy dog that a lady shouldn't be seen with."

All interest in the dog is lost when a scream is heard; it is a woman's scream. Leah kicks her horse and trots towards the source of the scream but Christine's horse isn't quite up to it and just plods along. Leah gallops over the crest of a hill and comes across a woman being attacked by four burly men armed with swords. She is very overweight and cannot run away, so the men push her to one another.

"Come ma'amoiselle, give us your money," says the first thug.

"Oh no, Jean," cries another thug who pushes the women away, "I think we should have a good time with her first."

The third thug pushes her away. "You must have lots of money, you're so well dressed."

The fourth thug catches the woman, then pushes her to the floor. "Now my lady, let me show you what a real man I am."

"STOP!" shouts Leah.

The four men turn to look at Lady Leah astride her white horse with her long blonde hair flowing down her back and shoulders, and her armour glistening in the sun. The fat woman looks up and gasps.

"Now what have we here, a lady Knight?" says the lead thug.

The four thugs laugh then draw their swords. Leah dismounts slowly and walks forward a few paces then holds out an outstretched right arm with open fingers without looking in the direction of her outstretched arm.

"Squire, my sword."

No reply, she turns around slowly and there is no sign of Christine, just Lady Leah's horse standing there. The first thug charges with his sword held over his head but he is stopped short when an armoured gloved fist slams into his chin. The weight of the sword pulls him down to the ground. The other three thugs stand there with their swords drawn, hesitant and afraid of this woman knight. But they are men and cannot let a mere woman get the better of them and they must prepare to fight her. Leah knows this and thinks back to when she was training with her father.

She is back in the castle grounds back in Lygeton with her father, neither have any weapons.

"Fighting is more than just swinging your sword around," declares her father. "Now come on, let us dance."

Father takes his daughter's hands and starts dancing, very gracefully thought a young Leah. She is on the verge of puberty, she wants to fight but her father is making her dance.

"Why are we doing this, Daddy?" she asks.

"Come on," he replies, "a step to the left." Except he steps to his right because it is the opposite way round to Leah's left.

"A step forward."

Again he steps back to allow his daughter to move forward.

"And a step to the right."

For many years Leah has practiced these stepping-type dance moves until she too was as graceful as her father. So graceful was she that one evening she is dancing but unaware her father is watching. He spies a bottle of wine which he picks to look at and has an idea.

"Who took some wine out of this bottle?" he bellows as he steps out of the shadows, surprising his daughter.

Leah knew father liked his wine and to take his drink was a crime most heinous. Father moves forward at lightning speed with his arms outstretched ready to grab Leah. But so graceful was she that all it took is a step sideways and a trip, the huge bulk of her father crashes to the floor.

"Father!" she cries. "I'm sorry."

She watches as her father's huge chest raises and falls repeatedly in a rhythmic manner, which then became a huge guffaw when he rolls over onto his back.

"Father?" she enquires.

He gets up and brushes his front.

"I wasn't really angry my dear," he says.

"No, then why…?"

"Why rush forward like that?"

"Yes."

"You were moving so gracefully and beautifully, I had to demonstrate what the dancing was about. And you executed the move perfectly."

He continues to laugh and he takes the bottle he was previously holding, pulls out the cork with his teeth and spits it out and then drinks a little wine. Leah feels pleased with herself.

Back in the present, the second thug charges with his sword held at head height – but Leah turns to her right and steps with her left foot before twisting so her back is to the charging man. The thug trips over Leah's outstretched angled right leg and crumples on the ground in a heap. The two remaining thugs look at each other and then charge either side of Leah in a classic pincer movement. They raise their swords and charge, but Leah gracefully steps out of the way to her left and the two men collide. Now there are four dazed men on the ground, gathering their senses Christine comes plodding over the hill. The four men clumsily get to their feet and scarper, leaving their swords behind.

Leah helps the fat woman up, who then brushes the dirt off her dress.

"Oui, allez-vous ens!" she shouts towards the running thugs.

"Merci good Knight," she says turning to Leah.

"You're welcome," replies Leah.

"Oh, you are English?"

"Yes, I am Lady Leah and this is my squire, Christine."

"Ooh mais oui, a good French name."

"Wot? Leah?"

"*Non*, Christine. It is a typical French name that has recently come into fashion."

"And madam, what is your name pray?" asks Leah.

"I am Madam Gaste-Viande and I am grateful to you"

"Why are you out here on your own?" asks Leah. "Surely someone of your stature should have an entourage?"

Madam Gaste-Viande brushes her dress some more

"I did have an entourage but the cowards ran off. They will be sacked when I get back home. Now where are you staying at the moment?"

"Nowhere really, we've just got here from the Middle East via Rome."

"Then you must come and stay with me at my castle and tell me of your travels."

Leah mounts her horse while Gaste-Viande grabs the horse's bits and leads them on.

"Where is your castle?" asks Christine.

"It is Chateau de Pieusse and is about five miles south of Carcassonne. We are not far from it."

In the distance is a rectangular building situated on a hill, although it doesn't have any towers it still has a moat and a drawbridge.

"It is my husband's castle." says Gaste-Viande.

"Is your husband there?" asks Leah.

"No, he died many years ago."

Gaste-Viande explains further as the troupe enters through the main gate.

"This castle is an ex-Cathar castle; many were slaughtered here in this building as part of their final extinction."

Christine gulps and looks around her.

"Don't worry," says Gaste-Viande. "I have heard no ghosts here."

They stop while a servant rushes into the courtyard and take the reins off Gaste-Viande. Leah and Christine both dismount.

"One of my servants will take you up to room where you may freshen up," says the hostess, "and we will eat in an hour's time."

Leah walks into her room.

"Yes, very comfortable. This will do nicely. Squire, my things."

But behind Leah there is no one.

"Christine? Where are you?"

In walks a pile of bags and weapons with two muscular legs protruding from underneath where her dress has been lifted up by Christine picking the items up. Christine drops everything on the floor and straightens out the hem of her dress so that her legs no longer show.

"Phew! That was heavy."

Christine turns her back to the bed and falls onto the soft mattress.

"Come on, we've got to get ready." Leah claps her hands together.

"Later, I want to sleep."

The hour passes and Leah walks into the room in a long crimson dress that shimmers in the light, with her hair tied up. Christine is in a long, green dress with yellow trim on the sleeves and neck.

"Now, that is more becoming," says Gaste-Viande.

Both the women curtsy in front their hostess. Presently all three are sat at a table while servants bring in food.

"There is plenty to eat, beef, pork, chicken... "

Christine cuts in.

"I'm vegetarian."

There is stunned silence.

"Madam," starts Gaste-Viande, "you are not a Cathar, are you?"

"No, I just don't like meat," replies Christine.

"Good, the Catholic Church comes down very hard on Cathars and they don't care who is with them."

"Don't worry," interrupts Leah. "We've been to see the Pope."

"Oh, so you've been to Avignon then?" enquires Gaste-Viande.

"Yeah, there as well."

"Yes, we saw the Pope in Avignon," says Christine.

"In Avignon?" asks Leah turning to her Squire. "Was that the Pope?"

"Yes m'lady."

"That guy on top of that rock?"

"That was the Rock of the Domes and is where the Pope's Palace is situated."

"When did the Pope go to Avignon and why didn't anyone tell me?"

"I did," said Christine under her breath.

"Never mind all that," interrupts Gaste-Viande. "Let us eat."

All three women tuck napkins into the necks of their dresses at the same time. Gaste-Viande picks up a piece of beef with her hands and bites into it. The meat juice runs down her chin, Leah does the same with a chicken leg, while Christine surveys the table.

"There's a pot of legumes," says Gaste-Viande with her mouth full.

Christine's eyes light up and she pulls the pot towards her. The vegetables float in a rich thick stock and quickly she uses a ladle to put a heap of vegetables on her plate.

"Besides, the Pope is French" says Gaste-Viande

"He didn't sound French," says Leah.

"That's because he spoke Latin," says Christine.

"Oh." Leah sits up straight. "And I suppose you speak Latin do you?"

"*Quidem*" replies Christine "*Intellexi omne verbum quod Papa sicut locutus est*"

"What?" Leah was genuinely surprised at her squire.

"*Unde enim scis illa nobilis est?*" asks Gaste-Viande.

"*Sic, certum.*"

"Oh come on you two, stop jesting with me, what are you saying?"

The two women just giggle.

Gaste-Viande continues the conversation, "So did you enjoy Avignon then?"

"Immensely. I loved the bridge of Saint Benezet" Christine says.

"Which bridge was that?" asks Leah.

"The bridge that spans the Rhône, that big long stone thing that snaked across the huge expanse of a river, the one that we saw from top of the Rock of the Domes."

"No, don't remember it." Leah tucks into a leg of chicken. Gaste-Viande speaks again.

"Now, tell me why you are travelling."

"We got banished from England by the king."

"For what?"

"Because I'm a woman." says Leah.

"I must say, it is unusual for a woman to be a knight, how did you become one?"

"I was the only child and my mother ran off with another man leaving me with my father. He taught me everything a knight needs to know, but he died."

"I'm sorry. Do you remember your mother?"

"I'm not sure," says Leah. "I think I do. If I bumped into her then I would probably recognise her. I was quite young when she left and my father never remarried. So you see, he passed everything on to me as there was no one else to pass it on to."

"And that's when the king banished you?"

"No." Leah takes another bite out of the chicken wing. "It's when I entered the annual joust at Dunstable and won it. The queen didn't like the idea of a woman knight so she convinced her husband to banish me for five years."

"When do you go back?"

"Well the five years is almost up."

"Do you English have a name for a woman knight?" asks Gaste-Viande.

"No," replies Leah. "Knights are mostly men and so a word was never invented for a female knight."

"A knightess I suppose," interjects Christine.

Both Leah and Gaste-Viande ignore the squire.

"In France, we have a name for a female knight. They are called *Chevalière*."

"You French are..." continues Leah "... so forward thinking. Maybe one day women will be equal to men here."

"Ooh, easy now. That's a bit too radical."

Gaste-Viande turns her attention to Christine.

"And what about you?"

"Eh?" Christine looks up with a mouthful of vegetables and broth dripping down her chin.

"How did you come about being a squire?"

"Well, my father was the village blacksmith in East Anglia and he taught me the metalworking trade. Although we were originally from Paddingatun, a village north-west of London, but when my mother died we moved up to Norfolk. When my father died I took over the business but the villagers didn't like having a woman for their blacksmith and brought in another. All the locals went to that blacksmith and my business dried up, so I packed my bags and left. Whilst travelling down the Icknield Way close to Warden Hills I came across Leah's castle, where she took me in and hired me as her squire."

All three women take another mouthful of food.

"Although," Christine continues, "I was kind of doing all right with my business, it's just that... "

"Yes?" enquires Gaste-Viande. "But what?"

"It's when I started to ask people for money to pay for the services they got a bit upset."

Gaste-Viande explains her situation.

"I used to be married to a rich man but he used to beat me for being fat."

"For being fat?" cries Christine.

"Yes," continued Gaste-Viande, "I couldn't help it, I love food."

With that she took another chunk out of her venison

"You see, he tried to starve me." She pauses.

"Starve me so that I could look thin, and be his trophy wife. However, he met with a... "

Here Madam Gaste-Viande just stares into space while holding her lump of venison. Then she sinks her teeth into the succulent piece of meat.

"... An unfortunate accident. His horse bolted and threw him off over into a precipice."

Leah and Christine have stopped eating and paying the utmost attention to Gaste-Viande.

"Well, I managed to convince him before he died to er... sign a will giving everything to me."

Madam Gaste-Viande suddenly puts down her food and screws up her face.

"Must be something to do with that young slut he wanted no one to know about."

She looks back to the other two women and smiles before taking a bite out of her venison. She speaks with a mouthful.

"I run a vineyard now and produce most excellent wine from this and I export all over Christendom. Now I am comfortable and enjoy my life, especially food. You must too, come on *mange, maintenent.*"

All three women tuck into their respective foods.

"Now," says Gaste-Viande, putting her lump of meat down and wiping her mouth with her napkin, "to business".

Leah and Christine turned to their hostess with their mouths full and holding their respective food.

"What business?" asked Leah.

"As you may or may not know, there is a melee coming up in Tornai in northern France."

"What's a melee?" asks Christine.

"It is a huge free-for-all fight with knights from all over Europe. The knights have to not only fight but capture another knight and hold him for ransom."

"Yes?" asks Leah.

"Well, Sir Girard will be there and I want to capture him."

"Who on earth is Girard?"

"He is the most feared knight in all of Europe."

Leah and Christine look at each other and say in unison. "Never heard of him."

"Not only would that be something, but for him to be captured by a woman. The whole of Europe would be speaking of this for years to come."

"What's in it for us?"

"A share of the prize."

Leah and Christine just stare at Gaste-Viande.

"Girard is incredibly rich and would pay handsomely."

"I'm in," said Leah.

"Oh not again!" moans Christine and takes another mouthful of vegetable stew.

By the end of the meal the servants start gathering up the plates. Christine lets out a little burp and apologises.

"Call that a burp?" says Leah and promptly lets out an enormous burp.

Leah has realised what she has done in someone else's home and apologises.

"That's not a burp," says Gaste-Viande, and produces the most ear-splitting, loudest burp anyone has ever heard that echoes throughout the castle for what seems like forever.

"That's a burp," she says with pride while the other two women sit there in awe.

"Now ladies," says Gaste-Viande ,"we must move and sit round the fire for a night cap before we retire to bed."

"I will join you in a moment, I need to feed Holdfast," says Christine.

"Oh, that mangy old dog you have outside," replies Gaste-Viande.

"Yes."

Leah and her host head towards the warmth of the fire while Christine makes her way to the kitchen to gather some scraps. The staff are helpful and provide Christine with a bowl and fills it with leftovers. Outside the door of the castle Christine appears, much to the joy of the dog, she places the bowl on the floor and the dog immediately tucks in, Christine strokes his back. The dog looks up at Christine with a sparkle in his eyes. Outside is very quiet, all that can be heard is Holdfast slobbering his food. The city of Carcassonne off in the distance is full of lights glimmering in the darkness. Christine turns to go back inside.

"Good night Holdfast," she says and disappears back into the castle, leaving the dog to enjoy his meal.

The three women sit around a burning fire giving its welcoming warmth, an orange glow flickering on the three faces. The servants bring in some hot drinks; a lavender tea for Gaste-Viande, a barley tea sprinkled with ground nutmeg for Christine and hot milk for Leah.

"Normally I would read now," says Gaste-Viande, "but what do you ladies do for entertainment?"

"Well Christine reads too," says Leah, she turns to her squire, "don't you?"

"Yes, I'm reading Clare of Assisi and the *Rule of Life*."

"Interesting?" asks Gaste-Viande.

"It's about how nuns should live their lives"

"I've heard nuns are so pious that they don't menstruate," continues Gaste-Viande.

"That's because they don't eat," replies Christine.

"Oh no, that wouldn't do for me," says Gaste-Viande, holding up a hand, "I love my food."

"Yes. But the book is all right I suppose, not as good as *Beowulf*."

"Ooh," cuts in Leah, "tell us about *Beowulf*."

"Yes, please do," adds Gaste-Viande.

"Well, *Beowulf* is an old Saxon story about a warrior of the Geats."

"Where's Geats?" asks Gaste-Viande.

"It's in Scandinavia. Anyway, he hears news that the villagers are plagued by a monster called Grendel."

The other two women sit quietly listening to Christine:

"Anyway, Beowulf kills Grendel in a great battle but Grendel's mother turns up and she is angry, but Beowulf being the hero type, defeats her too and the people make Beowulf king."

Leah adds, "Doesn't something happen to him?"

Christine continues, "Yes, the hero of the story fights another courageous battle with a dragon that he vanquishes, but unfortunately Beowulf is wounded, and he eventually dies."

The two listeners both go, "Aah."

"But he is given the greatest of burials that befits a king and a hero of his stature."

"That's a good story," says Gaste-Viande. "I like stories of great heroism and courageous deeds."

"Me too," says Leah.

"Now I've told my story…" Christine says as she pulls out from a bag a lute and hands it Leah.

Gaste-Viande starts clapping. "Yes yes, play the lute. I want to hear music," she squeals.

Leah starts playing melodies on her lute of both traditional music and her own compositions, while Christine taps out a rhythm on the tambourine. But to the surprise of the both women, Gaste-Viande gets up and starts dancing. Despite her huge size and the huge meal she has consumed, she is very graceful and moves as if she is floating on air. Although wanting to go to bed an hour earlier, the trio of women stay up until gone midnight enjoying themselves with music and dance.

The next morning Christine is fast asleep when she is woken up by Holdfast licking her face. Slowly she comes around and her vision comes into focus.

"Holdfast," says Christine as she quickly gets up, "you're not supposed to come into the castle."

She picks up her dog and runs downstairs in her nightdress with her bundle of fur and puts the little pet outside the main door, which she then slams shut. She quickly goes upstairs just as Leah is waking up.

"They're coming through the door, where's my sword squire?" she says blearily.

"There's no one coming through the door my Lady."

"But I just heard the door open. It is the enemy. My sword. Now!"

"No, that was just me putting Holdfast outside. Now come on and get up for breakfast."

Leah is starting to come to complete wakefulness.

"Ooh breakfast. I do hope our hostess has some black pudding."

Christine splashed some water over her face and pats it with a towel.

"Hardly," she says. "This is France, the food capital of the world."

"How can that be?" asks Leah, "with so much garlic in everything?"

***

Following breakfast Leah and Christine are training in the yard of Gaste-Viande's castle. Madam Gaste-Viande is in her chamber looking out at the two women doing their exercises; both the strong women have their arms exposed. She is thinking about the great riches they would obtain if Leah were to win.

"Oh, such riches," she thinks out loud.

Leah parries a blow from an overhead swing from Christine, sweat is pouring from both women's bodies.

"I must rest for a bit m'lady," says Christine. "I will go and bring some refreshment."

Christine puts her sword down and walks inside while Leah sits down while Holdfast gently strolls up to her; the little dog wags his tail furiously.

"Hello Holdfast," says Leah as she strokes the dog's head.

The dog sits down and leans against Leah's leg while Leah looks out to the countryside. She thinks the hilly landscape of Languedoc is beautiful and the city of Carcassonne in the distance, which makes her drift off. In her mind she is in the courtyard of her own castle. Her father's castle. He is there holding a sword and she is only eight years old.

"Come on my dear, pick up that sword," he tells her.

"But only boys fight," the little girl wails.

"Yes, but I don't have any boys, I only have you."

Leah tries to pick up the sword but it is heavy and she struggles with it. She drags it off the ground and the momentum continues the sword over her head, which brings her down. She lies on the floor with the hem of her dress splayed out over the floor, her arms stretched behind her head while still holding the sword.

"Perhaps that sword is a bit too big for you, try this." Father hands a smaller sword to Leah as she gets up which is easier for her to manipulate. Father takes a gentle swing with his sword, but little Leah move out of the way and drops the sword.

"What did you do that for?" he asks her.

"I don't want to get hurt."

"But only last week you wanted to play with swords. Come on let's try again."

Leah picks up the sword and this time she blocks the swipe from her father, but it knocks her off her feet.

"No, you must stand correctly, with your feet apart to be more stable."

Little Leah gets up and mimics her father's stance. Another gentle swipe is taken but this time Leah successfully blocks the blow.

"See, easy is it not?"

Little Leah nods.

Leah returns to reality as Christine walks into the courtyard, causing Holdfast to jump up and greet his mistress with a wagging tail.

"Aah Christine, please go and get my soap."

"Are you going to wash?"

"I wish to bathe in the river."

Christine rushes back inside while Leah heads down the hill towards the river in the bright sunshine. Holdfast is confused as to which woman to follow, but he just stands his ground and pathetically wags his tail. Leah takes off her clothes behind a bush, and steps into the cool water. Holdfast stands by the bank just barking. Leah sits down until just her head is showing with her hair sprayed out floating on the water, then Christine comes running down the bank with the soap.

"Ah Christine, bring the soap in."

"In? All right."

Christine steps behind the bush and undresses herself. She grabs the soap and runs into the river; Holdfast follows but stops at the water's edge.

"M'lady, your soap."

Leah starts washing herself, and then Christine starts splashing water over Leah.

"Stop that squire," she protests but starts splashing water back.

From a window up above in the castle, Gaste-Viande watches the two women at play.

"I do hope..." Gaste-Viande rubs her hands "... no-one walks past and sees this, I will be reported to the church for this."

She continues watching but deep down she is fascinated. She too would like to throw inhibitions to the wind and join them, but she must be modest. As all women should be modest. But...

She has an idea; she calls one of her servants.

"Servant, prepare some lunch and send someone to get the knight and her squire from the river."

"Tres bien, Ma'amoiselle"

Gaste-Viande turns to watch the two women again where Leah is having her back washed by Christine; she mutters to herself about what the villagers would think of these two naked women in the river, but she is unable to tear her gaze away from their beautiful bodies. At the moment the only audience they have is herself and the pigs in the pen by the bank. Although the pigs watch the two naked women, they are not interested; all that is going through their minds is the tasty turnips they are chewing on. Both women are well toned and have smooth, flawless skin. Gaste-Viande turns to Christine's body which has more muscles than a lot of men she knows, the muscles rippling in the late morning sunlight. She thinks about her own body, grabs a handful of belly and jiggles it up and down.

"Huh," she says out loud to herself. "Who wants to be thin and toned anyway, I love my food too much."

With that, she walks out of her room to towards the dining room.

Gaste-Viande is sitting at the table when Leah and Christine walk in.

"Ladies, time for lunch."

"I'm famished," says Christine.

"You haven't done anything," says Leah.

"How is your training going, madam?"

"Oh fine, I haven't lost any of my skills."

Christine is already tucking into some bread, cheese and onions.

"Good," says Gaste-Viande, "because we leave for the melee tomorrow."

"That's good; my squire will check and pack my things after lunch."

"Try some olives," says Gaste-Viande.

Leah puts an olive in her mouth but immediately spits it out across the room for it to hit one of the servants on the head. But being a servant he makes no movement or complaint.

"Yuk!" Leah cries, "I don't like olives."

Chapter 4

The Melee

All three women have travelled northwards through France. They eventually reach Tournai and set up their tent amongst the other knights and squires who themselves are from all over Europe; all view the three women with suspicion. The setting up of the tent is as usual left to Christine to accomplish while Leah just looks around, sizing up the competition. Madam Gaste-Viande declares she is off to register her knight and stumbles off; she stops at another knight's tent, looks around, picks up a chicken leg and walks off quickly before she is discovered. With the tent up, Leah sits down while her squire lays out the arsenal of weapons with Holdfast watching. After a while, the weapons are sorted and polished, the tent flap is flung aside and in walks Gaste-Viande.

"Bon, you are registered."

"I still think it's a mistake," says Christine polishing a sword.

"Nonsense," says Gaste-Viande, "it will be a great day to remember, what do you think, Lady Leah?"

"No problem," says Leah, and she takes another sip of wine from her goblet.

"Now," says Gaste-Viande, "where can we get some food from around here?"

"What happened to the food we brought with us?" asked Leah.

"Well..." stammered Gaste-Viande, "let's go get some, how you say *grub*."

"Oh ma'amoiselle, you didn't eat all the food?"

"I was hungry, *d'accord*?"

"Come," says Leah, putting her arm around Gaste-Viande's shoulders, "let's go and find some food."

"Ah, *c'est bon*."

"Just one catch though."

"*Oui*."

"You're paying."

Leah turns her head towards Christine behind her and smiles, Gaste-Viande's head drops.

"*C'est la vie*."

The three women walk through the evening camp: knights and their squires are everywhere sitting round fires, eating and drinking. No one can fail to notice three women walking through the camp. Word has got around that there are three women on their own with no men, the knights start jeering.

"Harlots!" they cry with more calls of "minxes"!

"*Avoirdupois*!" someone cries referring to Gaste-Viande's size.

Christine is getting agitated.

"I'll go and punch them," she says between her clenched teeth.

"No squire, you will stay with us," Leah tries to calm Christine down.

Another knight shouts out "strumpet"!

Leah loses her cool and turns but doesn't get any further as Christine has grabbed hold of her shoulder; Gaste-Viande also takes hold of Leah's free arm.

"Save it for tomorrow, my lady," says Christine into Leah's ear.

"Yes, remember they will respect you then," says Gaste-Viande.

The three women carry on until they find some food, now all their interest is on their supper and the cat calls no longer have any affect. The intrepid three return to their tent to feast and settle down for the night.

The next morning, crowds have gathered for yet another melee, all hoping it would be better than the year before and all hoping for that little bit extra violence than the year before. They are getting excited already and are baying for blood. Leah is astride her trusty steed while Christine hands her the various weapons. The field stretches out in front of them for what seems like miles, dotted here and there with a few trees. The landscape is flat and lonely villages can be seen from miles away.

"This is enormous," says Leah.

"Well, it was the biggest sword I could make that wouldn't be unwieldy," replies Christine handing over Leah's sword.

"No, I meant this..." Leah's hand sweeps across in front of her while Christine is still holding the sword "... the melee. We don't have anything like this."

Madam Gaste-Viande saunters over.

"*Tres bien*, we are ready *non*?"

"Which one is Sir Girard?" says Leah.

"That one over there." Gaste-Viande points with a half-eaten chicken leg which is watched intently by Holdfast.

"The one with the dark phizzog?"

"Phizzog?" Gaste-Viande looks confused. "*Quest-que ces't une phizzog?*"

"It's a face," replies Christine. "Phizzog means face. Leah is referring to the dark shadow on his chin."

"I know," says Gaste-Viande. "Typical of French men, so hairy ugh!"

She takes another bite from her chicken leg whilst Holdfast salivates down his hairy chest.

The knights gather on the field of which there are hundreds of them of different nationalities. The king of France is hosting the event, Philip VI of Valois, the Fortunate. He sits in his travelling throne with his entourage around him.

"Ooh, this dreadful heat," he says, "can't someone do something about this dreadful heat."

There are murmurs in his little gathering. Suddenly King Philip sits up.

"Ooh I say, I do so like the colours on that knight. I wonder who his colour co-ordinator is? I'll have to hire him to do my bedroom."

"Your majesty," says his squire, "it is time to start the games."

"Oh, I suppose so."

The king pulls out a laced handkerchief, stands up and drops the hankie which starts the fighting. Christine doesn't know whether to watch or hide her face.

"You're going to die," she says to Leah.

"Well, we've all got to go at some point."

And with that Leah draws her sword, holds it aloft then spurs Joust-a-lot on and they gallop into the seething mass of men and horses.

"There she goes," says Gaste-Viande.

"She's going to die," says Christine.

As Christine was saying that Leah whacked some unknown knight off his horse with her sword, who fell with a thud on the floor only to be immediately surrounded by other knights determined to get their prize. There was a mixture of styles of armour. Mostly it was chain mail but a few knights, mostly the wealthier ones, had the new full body plate armour. One of those in full armour received a hefty swipe from Leah's sword, dismounting the knight and clattering to the floor with an almighty crash. Because his armour was not well made, he wasn't very mobile and couldn't get up thus making him an easy target for another knight, who quickly had his ransom.

After much fighting, Leah spies Girard and heads towards him, whilst bashing a few other knights out of the way. Girard stands out from the rest of the knights on account of his height and distinctive helmet. It is of the old flat-top style but has two enormous curved metal horns sticking of either side with two slits for the eyes, as opposed to one long single slit like most other helmets of the time. He himself is laying into some poor individual in chain mail; the beaten knight drops his sword and turns to scarper.

"Come back here so that I may brain thee!" cries Girard holding his sword aloft.

Another knight thinks Girard is now undefended with his sword raised and tries it on. He rushes towards the French knight with his sword, but Girard was too quick and brought the hilt of his sword down on the unfortunate knight's head, causing disorientation. The knight drops his sword and staggers off to be immediately captured by another knight.

"Girard!" cries Leah, as she dismounts her horse. The French knight turns to face Leah.

"Ah, so you want to fight with me, I will make short work of you."

The two knights stare each other out and then charge at each other with a clash of swords.

"I don't know who you are," begins Girard, "but you are now my sworn enemy and are about to meet your demise."

The two clash their swords and after a while Leah is knocked off her feet and falls to the floor but she quickly does a roll and is back standing up in ready pose. She is glad her squire took careful notes of what the Italians did and designed her armour well.

The Frenchman says, "come on you horrible English knight, I will fight you some more."

More clashing of swords, but Leah loses hers after Girard whacks it out of her hand. Gaste-Viande and Christine are watching from the sidelines. Christine puts her hands over her eyes; she then parts her fingers on one hand to expose her eye so that she can see. Holdfast puts one of his paws across his face and whimpers. And all the time there is a steady stream of injured knights being carried off on litters to their tents, for treatment. Leah is now having another flashback in her castle. She is thirteen years old and sword fighting with her father, she is doing well or so she thinks. Father is just letting her get used to the feel of the larger sword; she parries effectively although she is continuously stepping back. Suddenly father whacks the sword out of her hand and the sword travels across the courtyard floor. Father holds his sword to Leah's throat.

"Where's your back-up weapon, my dear?" he asks her.

Leah looks puzzled. Father throws his sword in the same direction as Leah's sword. He raises his arms.

"I am unarmed," he says.

Leah seizes her chance and starts to make a movement towards her sword but, in a lightning flash, Father whips out a large knife and holds it in front of Leah's face.

"Always have a back-up in reserve, my dear."

Strapped to Leah's side is a mace which she quickly grabs just as Girard raises his sword. Leah swings the mace low to which Girard sees but realises he is in no position to do anything about it. The ball of the mace with its sharp points on it travel towards him, fear grips Girard and to him the mace travels in slow motion. Too late, the ball of the iron slams into the Frenchman's groin in a gap between the armour plates. The thick padding underneath prevents major damage but is not thick enough to stop the intense pain. The Frenchman's eyes water profusely. He grimaces in pain and drops his sword. Finally Leah has her prize and calls for her horse. She grabs a rope and ties it to the French knight's feet, grabs her sword and then climbs her horse. As she gallops off, Girard is dragged behind clanging as his limp body hits rough patches in the ground. Ahead of Leah are five menacing-looking knights; one's from Germany, another from Ireland, one is from Spain and judging by the quality and workmanship of their armour, the last two are from Italy. These knights realise Leah would be a good catch and so hope to try their luck on her, but she quickly manoeuvres her horse to do a sharp turn, causing the trapped knight behind her to swing round in an arc. The rope is up against the shins of the five knights who realise quickly and are about to be tripped and move out of the way. Unfortunately for them, Leah has spurred her horse on and Girard's helpless body is pulled through the feet of the five knights, knocking them over one by one.

"CLANG! CLANG! CLANG! CLANG! CLANG!"

All five knights are left sprawling on the ground, ready to be conquered themselves. Leah takes her captor to their rest area. As Leah gallops in Christine and Gaste-Viande are jumping up and down with joy while Holdfast runs round and round on the spot, chasing his tail. Leah dismounts and Christine drags the helpless knight into their tent.

Girard is coming round now and slowly Leah and Christine come into view, Christine walks out of the tent leaving Leah alone with the French knight. Leah takes her helmet off and her blonde hair falls out over her shoulders.

"*Mon Dieu!*" cries Girard, "*une femme.* I have been defeated by a woman."

"Yes, and this woman demands a high ransom for your release."

Leah puts her helmet on the table and picks up a goblet of wine, some of which she drinks. Girard is coming to his senses and tries to stand up, but stops immediately when he sees the point of a sword inches from his face.

"You will not try to escape sir, so you might as well make yourself comfortable."

Girard sits back down realising he doesn't have his armour on; he must have been stripped while unconscious.

"You are a very beautiful woman," says Girard.

"Forget it," says Leah.

"No, I mean it. I could make you very comfortable as my mistress."

"Hah!" cries Leah. "I'm not being anyone's mistress, I am in command of my own life."

Girard stands up and Leah immediately thrusts her sword in front of his face again

"Come now ma'amoiselle" says Girard with pleading hands in front of him, "there is no need for violence."

"Keep back," demands Leah, but Girard advances yet again.

"I am enthralled by your beauty, such a vision of loveliness."

Somebody clumsy outside, unknown to Leah and Girard, trips on one of the guy ropes holding the tent. The fabric of the tent wavers inside involuntarily causing Leah to move her eyes to see, not a huge movement but enough for Girard to move forward at lightning speed to knock the sword out of Leah's hand. Leah wastes no time in thinking about and immediately slams her fist into Girard's face.

"Ow Madame, that hurt. Please, may we talk about this?"

Christine with Holdfast in tow and Gaste-Viande, have tracked down Girard's squire, Arnoud. He is a short man with typical dark hair across his face but very little of it on his head. He is a devious little man holding an iron bar which he waves around when he feels the need to, then he looks up to the two taller women. There is a short exchange between them.

"This is outrageous, you cannot ask for that amount for the release of my lord."

"Nonetheless, that is what my lady is asking for."

"It is too much, I must speak with Sir Girard," he says, pointing the iron bar at Christine.

The squire walks away from the women

"*Excuse-moi* Arnoud," says Gaste-Viande, "our tent is this way."

Arnoud stops abruptly and turns around again pointing his iron bar.

"Humph," he says, and walks off in the direction Gaste-Viande is pointing.

Girard moves forward and puts his hand on Leah's shoulder, but that is as far as he gets because Leah has grabbed the hand, twists it and throws Girard on the floor. Girard gets up quickly and faces Leah.

"Madam, please... hurt me some more, I am enjoying this."

Leah swings her fist round in an arc right across Girard's face, knocking him to the floor.

"Oooh, the pain. You hurt me good ma'amoiselle, I would enjoy this if you were my mistress."

Arnoud is marching determinedly ahead while Christine and Gaste-Viande follow. He stops suddenly to turn and face the two women.

"Why am I doing deals with women?" he demands, waving his iron bar around.

"Well, sir," says Christine, "we have your lord and we won't release him until we get the ransom we ask for."

"Preposterous," he returns, and points the bar straight at Christine's face.

"Can you take that iron bar out of my face?" demands Christine.

"Why? You afraid ma'amoiselle?"

Christine looks into the Frenchman's eyes, beads of sweat trickling down his forehead. At lightning speed, Christine grabs the iron bar out of Arnoud's hand. She holds each end and pulls down on the bar until, slowly it starts to bend until it is a semi-circle. Christine drops the now useless weapon at Arnoud's feet. For a moment, just a tiny split-second moment, Arnoud shows fear in his face which wouldn't have been seen by a passer-by, but Christine and Gaste-Viande notice; as does Holdfast who starts barking at Arnoud.

"And now monsieur, if you would continue please," says Gaste-Viande.

Arnoud turns and continues his determined march again.

Girard holds out his right arm, Leah has a thought to counter the next attack, in her castle her father asks Leah to throw him over her body.

"But that's impossible, you're twice my weight," protests Leah.

"No it's not. Try it."

Father holds his arm out and Leah gingerly takes hold of it. She turns her body so her back is pressed against her father's and pulls on his arm. No matter how hard she pulled, Father's body wouldn't budge.

"Let me show you," he says, and his arm is released.

He takes Leah's arm and places it over his shoulder.

"Bend your knees thus," he says and performs his said action, "whilst pulling the opponent; that's you my dear," he smiles as he says this, "using the strength of your legs, straighten them."

This he does and raises Leah off the ground.

"Now you are off the ground now. What can you do?"

Leah moves her legs around; she could just touch the ground with her toes but without warning, father twists his body and Leah topples off her father's back and onto the floor.

"Now you try it," he says.

Again Leah grabbed her father's hand, pulls him forward, bends her knees and lifts his huge bulk off his feet. She turns slightly and father slides off Leah's back and onto the floor onto his back. He rolls over onto his side and props his head on his hand to see Leah smiling.

"See, it's easy, is it not?" he says.

Back in the tent, the Frenchman still has his arm outstretched only to have it grabbed by Leah; she pulls him hard against the back of her body, twists and hurls the huge mass of the Frenchman over and onto the table. The table breaks and its contents go flying.

"Ma'amoiselle love me some more."

Girard is by the tent flap surrounded by broken wood and has an opportunity to flee, much to the horror of Leah. But instead he hurls himself at Leah – who steps to one side whilst holding out a straight leg, tripping up the knight. He falls flat on to the front of his body but quickly turns to one side, splits his legs and then clamps them closed again on Leah's legs. He twists slightly and Leah falls to the floor, she turns over on to her back but it is too late, Girard is standing astride her again.

"And now ma'amoiselle..." he starts but never finishes as he doubles over due to a lightning-fast armoured foot into his groin.

"Not again," he murmurs and drops to the floor.

Leah stands up with her hair dishevelled just as Christine, Gaste-Viande and Girard's squire comes in. They look at the stuff strewn across the floor and Girard lying there unconscious. The squire rushes to his master.

"My lord!" he cries as he lifts up Girard, "what has happened here?"

Girard arouses into consciousness.

"My, what a woman," he blurts.

"My Lord, my Lord! These people demand a huge ransom for your release. It's preposterous. They are only women; we could easily make our escape."

Girard gets up uneasily.

"My faithful squire, we could no more escape from this..." he pauses.

"... This amazon. Pay them; pay them what they ask for."

With that, Arnoud runs out. Girard turns to Leah and bows; he takes her hand, kisses it and says, "Ma'amoiselle, you have won the fight fairly. I applaud you and any time you want another fight, please visit me at my home in Bayeux."

Girard stops to stroke Holdfast, and then limps out as his squire comes back in with a wheelbarrow filled with three sacks full of coins.

The trio have gone off to fetch some more food and walk through the camp again. Through the camp there is a variety of entertainment; jesters and troubadours, bears shackled up and something catches Christine's eye. An archery stand! She has a go and wins every prize, they continue on their way to find food. But there are no catcalls, no insults. The whole camp knows about Lady Leah and her capture of the greatest knight in all Europe. Now they just shout "well done" or "oh brave lady knight". Some even cheer and clap for Lady Leah.

"That's better," says Leah, "much more civilised."

"We did tell you," says Christine.

"Where's the food?" asks Gaste-Viande.

The sun has set and the three women are sitting in their tent, eating their evening meal. Leah has her ale and Christine drinks her mead while Gaste-Viande has her wine. They haven't forgotten Holdfast who happily and noisily laps water from a bowl.

"We are rich," says Gaste-Viande, as all three turn their heads to look at the pile of cash in the corner (as does Holdfast). The three women chink their mugs together.

"Thank you Gaste-Viande," says Leah, "but we must be going to England tomorrow. You must come and visit."

"And I must return to my castle in Languedoc, I have a vineyard to look after and I'd like to sell a wine that rivals that from Bordeaux."

"And we..." Leah is momentarily thoughtful "... must visit the king to ensure we can return to England."

"*Oui*, but first we enjoy ourselves. A toast to the greatest female knight in Europe."

All three raise their goblets, then quaff their drinks.

"And now, a song," says Leah with her lute.

Joust-a-lot
Has got a lot
But Swiftflight
Is not right

"Hey, that's not fair," says Christine. "Swiftflight is a lovely horse."

All three women descend into fits of laughter.

Chapter 5

The Green Fields of England

The intrepid pair have reached Calais looking for passage to their beloved England. Leah is waiting on her horse but is not wearing her armour for the journey (if the ship sank she would sink with it). She is holding the reins of her squire's horse as she views the harbour which is a mass of activity and of sound and she is amazed that, amongst this activity, there is actually order and things happen smoothly. She looks across the sea and spies in the distance the White Cliffs of Dover when Christine comes walking back with Holdfast following close behind.

"I've managed to get us passage on a Hansa ship, it goes to Dover. It does also go straight to London but I thought Dover would be good enough."

Christine holds up a piece of parchment.

"Why not? We can afford it. We're rich now," replies Leah.

"Sssh my lady. We don't want every vagabond and cut-throat to know, do we? We are poor travellers coming back from pilgrimage."

Lady Leah dismounts and the two women guide their horses to the edge of the harbour.

"There's our ship," points Christine to a single-masted ship. "That's what's known as a cog."

Bobbing up and down in the waves next to it is another ship with an extra mast.

"Why couldn't we go on that ship?" Leah points.

"Because it's more expensive."

"Oh yes. We're poor."

The captain comes over.

"You two ladies going to Dover?" he says in a germanic accent.

"Yes we are," replies Leah.

"Just take your horses up the gang plank and make yourselves comfortable somewhere."

"Thank you Captain."

By now the captain's attention was elsewhere and he starts to move off towards the ship.

"*Schweinhund!*" he cries, "belay that rigging you *dummkopf.*"

"All right Christine, let's go," says Leah.

***

Leah guides her horse up the gangplank but she doesn't hear another set of hooves behind her. Turning round she sees

Christine pulling at the reins of Swiftflight, who refuses to budge.

"Come on squire!" calls out Leah.

"I don't think she wants to come."

"Well, I don't care how you do it, just get that damn horse on this ship."

"There's no need to swear, my lady."

The captain has come over to Christine but Leah can't hear what they are saying to each other.

"It's all right, the captain has a solution, cost a bit more though," says Christine, coming up the gangplank.

"Where has the captain taken your horse?" asks Leah.

"You'll see in a moment."

Another few minutes and then...

"There," points Christine, to a horse in the air, "they are using the harbour crane."

The horse swings about while she neighs at her discomfort, her legs dangling below her body. The ropes creak under the strain of the horse, the armour and the mementos.

"Where's your dog?" enquires Leah.

"I don't know." Christine cups her hands and shouts "Holdfast"?

Leah mutters whilst looking in the opposite direction, "I'm not with her."

Then Christine notices a little head pop up from inside the baggage on the back of Swiftflight; he barks.

"There he is," says Christine pointing.

"Good. Perhaps we can now get going," says Leah, walking away to find a comfortable spot, while Swiftflight is put under the awning along with Joust-a-lot and two other horses.

***

The mooring ropes have been pulled in enabling the ship to get under way, Christine sits down next to Leah and Holdfast joins them, the dog rests his muzzle on Christine's legs. Many people are milling about on the deck of the ship while a few others are standing by the edge watching as the ship pulls out of harbour. The squire pulls out another home-made device.

"I've learned to use a lodestone," she proudly declares. "They use them to steer ships at sea, like this."

Christine holds it under Leah's face whose eyes open. She stares at the stone swinging to and fro at the bottom of its string. Leah grabs the gadget and throws it overboard, she hears a satisfying splosh.

"Now, I want a kip so be quiet, squire."

"Yes my lady," replies Christine.

Holdfast looks up without moving his head and whimpers.

Leah drifts off and thinks of her home in England, she imagines she is with the king who declares that the country is at war with France.

"Lady Leah," the king addresses her, "is your army ready?"

"Yes," Leah replies, and holds out her hand towards her knights.

Standing before the king is an army of women knights with their long hair flowing down their backs and shoulders.

"They are fine-looking knights," declares the king; with him is his queen who nods in agreement. Leah draws her sword and raises it in the air; the female knights do likewise and shout.

"My army is ready to battle for you, your majesty," declares Leah.

"Then go forward," declares the king.

The female knights charge forward and clash with the enemy who are dispatched easily by Leah's army of women.

Leah is abruptly awoken by Christine.

"My lady, we are coming into Dover."

"I was having a nice dream then," Leah says sleepily. "Ah! Women in armour."

Christine stands up, Leah holds out her hand and Christine pulls up her lady.

"Talking of armour, I'm going to put mine on, help me squire."

The ship's crew throw their ropes to the pier which are caught by the men who pull the ship closer.

"Can you see that, my fine squire?" asks Leah.

"What's that m'lady?"

"The green fields of England."

"And the cold, and the damp."

"Hush now," Leah scolds Christine. "We are in England now."

Leah turns to face Dover port as the gangplanks are put in place. Dover castle sits high on the cliff top.

"But you are right; I did like the warmth of southern France."

Leah guides her horse to the gangplank while Swiftflight is ignominiously transferred by crane again. Leah takes advantage of her arrival and raises her hands high, her armour glistening in the sun with her brilliant, white horse standing behind her.

"Hello England. Lady Leah is back," she cries out.

However, her triumphant return is ruined by hordes of people rushing down the gangplank knocking Leah, she loses her normal coolness.

"Hey, what's the hurry? I am a lady you know, give me some respect."

"Sorry m'lady," says Christine. "They're pilgrims. Probably going to Canterbury or Saint Albans."

"Yes well, they should learn some manners. Now where do we go?"

"We have to find Watling Street which takes us all the way to London, but first we need to find where the crane is, that's where Swiftflight will be."

The two women are now standing on sound ground holding the reins of their horses. Leah in her full armour and looking resplendent, Leah wants to make a grand return back into England.

"Finally we're here," says a disgruntled Leah.

"I can't help it if Swiftflight doesn't like gangplanks."

The two women mount their horses with Holdfast sitting between Christine's legs on the horse. He barks triumphantly.

"Right," says Leah, "let's go."

The grand return of the intrepid travellers was soon marred by typical English weather. Along Watling Street a good few miles from Dover, the sky darkens and then the heavens open up. Leah puts her helmet on and, although the noise of the rain pounding her armour causes irritation, she was glad that she was dry. On the other hand, Christine had no protection and she became soaked and cold. Holdfast fared a little better, even though he was exposed to the elements, he could snuggle further into Christine and at least get some body warmth. The night draws in to further darken the sky.

"I'm cold my lady," wails Christine.

"Come on, you're English. Able to withstand the harshness of the world. Proceed henceforth."

Christine starts to shiver.

"Can't we stop somewhere, m'lady?"

"We need to press onward towards our goal."

"But I'm cold, wet and hungry," grumbles Christine.

Suddenly a wolf's howl is heard.

"I don't think we should be out here in the dark with those wolves prowling around," stammers Christine.

"We'll be able to dispense with them," replies Leah.

A brief flash of a pair of eyes is seen.

"They're very close," says Christine.

Holdfast lets out a bark and off in the distance is a glow of a residence of some sort. As they get closer it is a tavern with its welcoming light hanging up outside, a crumbly old wattle and daub building with a thatched roof.

"We'll stop here," says Leah.

"It looks as though it could do with demolishing," says Christine.

"Are you complaining? We could move on elsewhere."

Christine turned slightly and looked at the rain coming down heavily.

"No, we'll stay here."

The horses are quickly taken into some stable and locked away from the predators and Christine would like to lodge here for a night. She enquires about lodging for the night then takes everything off the horses upstairs to their room. The shutters are banging in the wind, rain blowing in through the open window. Christine reaches out of the window to grab the shutters and the lights glints on a wolf's eyes looking up at her. She quickly closes the shutters and fastens them to stay closed. Leah takes her armour off and wears her under-armour garments.

"Let's get something to eat," says Leah, and the two walk downstairs into the main saloon.

The barmaid asks "What would you like to drink?"

"A mead for my friend and ale for me," Leah gives her order.

"Where are we?" Christine asks the barmaid.

"Canterbury is just two miles in that direction," she points the same way that Leah and Christine have been travelling.

"Oh good, not far from London then?"

"Oh, you're not on pilgrimage to Canterbury then?"

"No, but we could pop into the cathedral on the way," says Leah.

"Oh, could we?" asks Christine.

"All right," says Leah. "I know you want another memento."

Leah turns to the barmaid and asks, "Do you do food?"

The serving wench replies that they do.

"All right, I'll have salted pork."

"With bread?" asks the wench.

"Yes."

"And can you do a pot of hot vegetable stew?" asks Christine.

"You're not one of them funny vegetarians are you?"

Leah cuts in. "She's far from funny, she never makes me laugh."

All three women start laughing.

"All right luvvies, I'll go and get your food," says the bar wench.

Christine and Leah both express their gratitude.

"Come on my lady, let's go and sit in front of the fire and dry out."

The pair are now a lot warmer when their food arrives, which they devour with relish.

"At least there's no garlic in this food," says Leah.

No reply from Christine, she is too busy eating. They have forgotten their chills as they sit in their high-backed chairs; Holdfast is sitting on Christine's lap also enjoying the warmth. The alehouse is practically empty with no one around because of the bad weather. A couple of monks enjoy a drink together at the bar (presumably on pilgrimage) whilst two farm workers enjoy a game of dice seated at a table in the middle of the room. Both Christine and Leah are tired, but Christine reads a book whilst Leah drifts off.

Leah is back on her travels, on this occasion it is in Makuria in North Africa where she and Christine visited and stayed. The villagers had little but they welcomed the pair in and gave what little food they had. They were under constant threat from the Mamluk Sultanate from further north. It was mostly religious in nature, the villagers being Christian and the attackers were Muslim. On many attacks from a small army, Leah single-handedly defended the village (with help from her squire) which inspired the villagers to fight back themselves using farming implements as weapons. Christine being a superb archer would initially dispense with the first row of attackers, and then both women would charge into the mass of soldiers and hack their way through. The villagers on seeing this would pick up any farm implements to hand and fight with those. However, the Muslim invaders soon came to respect Lady Leah, their general being told by his aide, "Sire, the devil woman is defeating our army. See how the villagers rise up against us."

"Yes," said the general, "invigorating, isn't it?"

The ongoing fighting eventually led to admiration causing the two armies to sit down to peace talks. Feeling she had accomplished something worthwhile she left the villagers feeling happy. She wakes up and sees Christine still reading.

"Time to retire to bed, methinks," says a weary Leah.

Christine closes her book and the two tread wearily upstairs.

The next day, feeling refreshed and continuing their journey, Leah and Christine have reached Southwark and across the river they see the seething mass that is London. Dominating the skyline is Saint Paul's Cathedral standing proud. They both cross London Bridge which itself is an entire village of shops, homes and even a chapel. They enter into the city of London but are glad they are sitting on their horses; below them is mud everywhere except that it isn't mud of the wet earth variety. They see people around them and what is being thrown onto the floor. Butchers throw animal remains out of their shops, as do fishmongers who throw out fish-heads. Buckets of human waste are thrown out of windows above them, houses of sometimes three storeys tall. People meander through the crowded narrow streets mashing this mixture of the sum total of London waste. Cattle and pigs also share the streets with humans – not even bothering to stop to eliminate their own bodily wastes. Some people try in vain to wash away the filth with buckets of water but to no avail, the muck stays put.

"Phworr! What a smell," says Leah.

"Yes well m'lady, we are in London now," says Christine.

The pair head to the inner depths of the city.

"We need to get to Westminster," says Leah.

"That way," points Christine.

Leah holds her hand to her head.

"Ooh," she moans.

"Headache?" says Christine.

"Yes," replies Leah, "it must be this foul air, there must be an apothecary nearby."

"I know where there is one; we have to go this way."

Christine turns her horse around and Leah follows suit, the two horses trudge through the city mud until they reach King William Street.

"There's one," cries Leah, "down there on Shiteburn Road."

"That's no good," cries Christine.

"Why?"

"Because it doesn't have a sign to say that it belongs to the Guild of Saint Luke. Should be closed down really."

Christine urges her horse on.

"I just want to get rid of this headache," cries Leah, who then gets her horse going too.

"I know a good apothecary just round the corner," says Christine.

Leah shouts on, "I should be in front."

Christine turns round, "you want your headache cured, yes m'lady?"

"Yes" says Leah feebly.

The intrepid pair continue up Cheapside until they reach a side street called Gutter Lane.

"Are we there yet?" demands Leah.

"Yes, I'll go get the herbs," Christine continues but turns around on her horse.

"There's an alehouse just there, I will meet you in there."

As Christine's horse slowly walks away laden down with weapons, armour, mementos and a dog, Leah is aware someone is watching her. She turns and looks down at a group of people standing and staring at her.

"A lady knight." they whisper amongst themselves without breaking their stare at Leah.

"What you lot looking at?" Leah demands and then spurs her horse onwards to Ye Olde Cock Inn.

Christine has arrived outside the apothecary named "Pestle and mortar".

"An original name," mutters Christine as she ties up her horse, lifts Holdfast off and onto the ground then they both go into the shop. As the door opens it knocks a parrot on its perch above which caws loudly, at which Holdfast barks. Christine stands in the middle of an average-sized room filled with all sorts of curiosities – rows and rows of jars are filled with powders and finely chopped leaves. There are strange animals pickled in jars and bunches of twigs with their leaves or berries still attached hanging from the ceiling. The smell is overpowering but not unpleasant, thinks Christine, although Holdfast finds it a little uncomfortable with his sensitive nose. Christine looks into one of the jars.

"My God," she thinks, "it's a pickled baby."

But on further inspection she realises it's just a monkey. Looking at a jar on the shelf below she sees a jar with a giant eye in it. Then it blinks.

"Huh?" Christine moves back a bit.

The eye moves to the side to reveal Holdfast's face. Christine quickly realises the liquid in the jar magnified her dog's eye and starts to chuckle.

"Holdfast," she says "stop messing about."

The dog wags his tail but turns his head to the direction of the counter. Christine hears a chuckle coming from the back somewhere, "Ha ha ha!"

A woman appears through a door from a room which is attached to the back of the shop. She is holding a pestle and mortar and grinding something. She stops and looks up, the two women hold each other's gaze for a moment. Christine speaks first.

"Hello Mildred."

Mildred puts down her pestle and mortar and puts on a pair of spectacles.

"Ha ha ha, Christine!" she exclaims with joy which quickly turns to a mock scolding. "Where have you been?"

"I've been travelling," says Christine moving forward. "All across Europe with my Lady Leah."

Mildred is a short woman with Mediterranean looks, possibly Italian or more likely Greek.

"We've just come from France where we have made our fortune. Leah captured some famous knight called Sir Girard."

"I know not that name," replies Mildred.

"No, nor me until we got to the Melee."

"Ha ha ha, what a lovely dog."

Holdfast moves forward a bit sensing that this is a friendly human so that Mildred can stroke his head.

Lady Leah approaches the alehouse, a typical building of the time attached to all the other typical buildings, dark wood with white plaster in between. The top storey overhangs but is supported by timber posts, to which Leah ties her horse to. She walks through the door into a dimly lit room, the only light coming in through the window at the far end which has an oiled-soaked parchment hanging to keep out the wind. The house is full of dirty-looking men sitting in two groups one each side of the room; some of the men have wenches with them sitting on their laps. Leah turns around to face the bar and orders a mug of ale; the barman pours out the drink into a flagon and hands it to his customer. Leah pays with some coins from a pouch hanging from her belt around her waist and then turns around; she sits down at a solitary table in the middle of the room. Leah takes a sip when she hears a voice behind her.

"What have we here?" demands the voice of a man, "a lady knight?"

Leah, still with the flagon at her lips, slowly puts her drink down.

"An abomination, I would say," the man continues.

Leah slowly stands up, still holding her mug of beer, and turns to face the lowlife who had just insulted her.

"Methinks..." continues the man, "that I should show you that you are just a woman and should know your place."

He holds his crotch as he says this. Another man stands up behind Leah and kicks away the table she had just been sitting at.

Leah holds out her free arm and says, "Squire, my short sword if you please."

The room of people erupt into laughter and Leah realises that Christine is not here.

Leah knows this man will rush her. She thinks back to her days in the castle with her father. She is eighteen years old and nearly as tall as her father. He grabs her hand and places it on his chest.

"Now, hold me back," he tells her and moves forward.

Leah is unable to hold the full weight of her father back, she is pushed back herself. He stops pushing and laughs. Leah drops her hand but finds her father's hand on her chest above her breasts.

"Father, what are you doing?" she protests.

"Now push forward," he says.

Leah expects to stay put as she knows the strength of her father but pushes as hard as she can. Unexpectedly, her father withdraws his hands very quickly and she propels herself forward uncontrollably. She topples but her father catches her arm before she falls.

"You see," he continues, as Leah straightens herself up, "you don't use force against a much greater force. You use their force."

Her father smiles and shows his pristine white teeth.

"Make sure they are committed to their action, then just step out of the way and let them do the rest."

It was so simple, thought Leah. As if he read her mind, Father bursts out laughing.

"Now my dear, let me show you what a man I am," says the unknown assailant in the pub.

He moves forward towards Leah forcibly but he finds Leah's hand has gripped the front of his shirt. The movement of the man didn't need much extra force to propel him violently forward as Leah steps to her left, and then she lets go, just as her father had shown her. The man, with so much momentum, continues into his companion who was behind Leah, and the two men are thrust into another man sitting down who is with two women. The two thugs crumpled on the floor but quickly recompose themselves and stand up. The third man is not happy and he himself stands up. He towers above the two men, who are knocked together by the large man; they fall to the floor unconscious. The tall man returns to his seat and his women.

Back in the apothecary Christine is making her request
"I need a headache cure for Leah."

"Ha ha ha, how about some lavender leaves? You just steep them in hot water and... "

"No" cuts in Christine, "she doesn't like lavender. Have you got something else?"

"Well..." Mildred puts her forefinger on her chin and then holds it up in the air.

"There's Belladonna, much more powerful, guaranteed to cure any headache."

"Yes," says Christine, "deadly nightshade, she'll love that one. I'll take some."

"Ha ha ha."

By now, the rest of the alehouse has decided they are all going to take on Lady Leah. Two bunches of men either side of Leah are slowly moving towards her menacingly. Leah quaffs the last of her ale and tosses the flagon to one side. The tall man is gripping his two wenches but is also watching the proceedings with interest. A man breaks free from one of the groups to Leah's left. She drops to one knee while turning to her left and rams her fist into the man's stomach. She doesn't withdraw her fist but instead grabs the man's clothing and immediately stands up. The man's momentum continues up and over Leah's head, and he is propelled into the group on the opposite side, scattering the little collection of men over the floor. Leah doesn't waste the energy by stopping but continues to turn whilst stepping back. She rams her moving right elbow into the nearest man's face. He is off balance and falls into his own group, scattering the men there.

"Hmm... men," says Leah, as she returns to a relaxed pose with her hands on her hips.

She raises a clenched hand with an outstretched forefinger and shouts "barman, another ale please."

Christine slips the package into her bag and then turns to Mildred.

"So, what's the word on the street?"

Mildred has no hesitation in replying.

"The King of England has declared himself King of France too."

"That will upset the present King of France. The two countries will probably end up fighting."

"Ha-ha good for business. There'll be more ill people around." Mildred rubs her hands.

"What else?"

"The king is adding some more to his palace."

"Westminster Palace? Oh we're on our way there."

"I believe," Mildred pauses, "ha ha that he is to dedicate it to Saint Stephen."

"Anything else?"

"All right all right," says a slightly agitated Mildred. "I understand what you're trying to get at."

"Yes? Well?"

"The whole of London knows you are back. They've known quite a while that you two were exiled."

"And...?"

"And what?"

"How do they feel about us coming back?"

"Mostly disgusted. I think they would like you two to stay away forever. However, I see many patients here and secretly, especially the women, they admire Lady Leah. They wish there were more lady knights. But you know what people are like, they just follow the crowds. They can't be seen to like anything different, can they? Ha ha ha!"

Leah didn't see the man behind rushing her but she heard him and dropped to one knee, causing the man to trip over her body. With perfect timing she stood up and the man somersaulted across the room and landed on one of the piles of men. She then turned round to be confronted by a row of three angry-looking men. She swung her right fist in a large arc and it connected with the chin of the first man, then the second man and then the third. All three were knocked senseless and fell into the other pile of dazed bodies. She then swung round holding up her clenched fist to confront the next man. He was a small-framed man with a slight hunch and holding a flagon of ale. It was the barman with Leah's order and he was shaking slightly.

"Your ale, madam," he stammered.

Leah immediately released her fist.

"Aah, thank you barman," as she hands some coins over from her belt pouch. "Keep the change."

Christine walks into the alehouse with Holdfast but both stop and survey the scene, bodies of dazed men lying in heaps on the floor moaning and groaning. Leah spots her squire and raises her flagon.

"Aah Christine, do come in and quaff some ale with me."

Christine walks towards the table in the middle of the room and sits down.

"Barman, a drink for my squire if you please," says Leah.

"You've been fighting," says Christine.

"Yeah so? You are going to tell me off?"

"No, I wanted to see it. How dare you have a fight without me knowing about it?"

"Yeah, and you missed it," Leah says, as she pokes Christine with her flagon. "It was a good fight."

Leah turns to the tall man by the window and raises her mug. The man responds in kind with a smile on his face. A moan is heard from one or other of the piles of bodies every so often. Holdfast jumps on one of the pile of bodies nearest to the window and jumps up and down on them and barks.

"Listen" says Christine. "I've got some Belladonna for your headache."

"Oh, I don't need it now, the headache's gone." Leah sips some more ale as the barman puts down a mug on the table for Christine. Leah puts her mug down and gets out some money for the barman who goes away, very happy.

"I have heard..." says Christine, "that Edward has declared himself King of France."

"Hmm... there's sure to be a war, I could offer my services to his army."

"Edward would never allow that."

"Well, we have got more important matters. Our return from exile needs to be confirmed."

The two ladies gulp some more ale down in unison.

Coming out of the alehouse, Leah and Christine mount their respective horses with Holdfast being mounted on Swiftflight. Holdfast barks forward and the pair start a slow meander through the grimy streets of London. They stop by a crowd of people in a small square. Being so high up they can see what is going on. A man is sitting down while a barber is examining his leg.

"I've an ingrown toenail," says the patient.

The barber looks closer at the nail. He slides his hand up the man's leg carefully inspecting the skin.

"It's more than your toenail," announces the barber.

"What?" says the man.

"It's your leg, it's diseased. It will have to come off."

"No," says the patient, "not my leg."

"Well, if it doesn't come off, it will be your life. That will be five pence please."

"That's expensive," says the man handing over some coins.

"Not for your life it isn't."

The barber puts the coins away in his pouch then hands the patient a bottle of ale.

"Here drink this" says the barber.

"I don't think I want to watch this," says Christine to Leah.

"Why not?"

"Because he is going to chop off that man's leg."

"Whatever for, he's only got an ingrown toenail."

"Because that barber is a butcher... come on, let's go."

The pair ride off as a scream is heard from where they have just been, and a cheer from the crowd.

"One day we won't have to rely on such barbaric practises," says Christine.

Leah replies, "Yes, and one day women will be equal to men."

Leah and Christine trot past Saint Paul's, then Fleet Street over the River Fleet. This became the Strand and was more countrified, they had left the city. They head south to the city of Westminster and towards Westminster Palace, a large oblong building with some scaffolding at one end.

"That's to be Saint Stephen's Tower," declares Christine.

There are a few buildings near the palace, the most prominent being Westminster Abbey, the rest of the area being fields. The palace sits on the bank of the River Thames.

"Here we are," says Leah, and the two women dismount.

"You know, this place was built by King Canute," says Christine.

"Who's Canute?" asks Leah.

"A Danish king from before the Normans."

"Danish, huh?"

With the horses tied up Christine ties the dog, too.

"I'm afraid Holdfast that dogs are not allowed in the palace."

Holdfast whimpers as the two women walk to the entrance.

Leah and Christine walk down a long hall, the main sound coming from the clink of Leah's armour. Leah stands in front of the king while his queen sits to one side with a disgusted look on her face.

"So, you have returned?" asks the king.

"Yes, my five years is up, I have been punished, now let me live at my castle."

"Hmm!" says the queen.

"Now my dear, their punishment is up."

"May I remind you," interrupts Leah, "my father fought and died for you."

"Yes he did," replied the king, suddenly realising he owed Leah a lot more than he was letting on.

"He was the best," adds Leah.

"My dear, her father fought during the Despenser Wars, I must lift the exile."

"Let them face the challenge if they want to stay," she replies.

"Oh yes, the challenge."

"What challenge is that your majesty?" enquires Leah.

"It seems we have a dragon terrorising the countryside, somewhere near Bedford I believe. If you want to stay, slay the dragon."

"All right," says Leah without hesitation.

"Don't be so cocky," says the queen turning in her seat towards Lady Leah, "many knights have tried and failed."

"I have seen many dragons on my travels, your highness."

"So, it's settled then? For me to pardon you, you will slay the dragon?" says the king

"By my troth I will your majesty," says Leah, she bows, turns and walks away with her squire. The king calls out.

"Lady Leah?"

Leah turns and faces the king, "Yes your majesty?"

"That is a fine suit of armour you have there."

The armour glistens in the light of the palace.

"Thank you your majesty, my squire made it."

Both women bow and then walk out.

Outside Holdfast is overjoyed to see his mistress, she picks him up and puts the dog on the horse's back with his short tail wagging furiously, and the pair untie their horses and mount them.

"Do you think you can meet the challenge?" asks Christine.

"Of course I can. I'm Lady Leah of Lygeton. Now, we need to find Watling Street."

"Oh, we have to go back to London."

"Ugh!" says a disgusted Leah.

Chapter 6

Back Home

Lady Leah and her faithful companion have journeyed many miles to Lygeton, which they get to by journeying up Watling Street. Normally they would continue up to Dunstable and then turn right onto the Icknield Way, but Leah wants to see Lygeton first and so they take a detour along a small, muddy road. As they enter the town there are many new buildings and lots of old burnt-out remains of other buildings. Leah stops her horse and asks a peasant:

"Say peasant, what has happened here?"

"Lygeton burned to the ground my... "

The peasant pauses as he realises he is talking to a lady knight.

"My lady... why, it's Lady Leah. You have returned."

The peasant smiles exposing many missing teeth.

"Never mind that, what happened here?" she reiterates her question.

"Since you left all them years ago, we've had marauding gangs stealing our belongings. Then when they couldn't steal anymore because we didn't have nuffink, they... "

The peasant voice croaked under the strain.

"They set light to the town."

"When did this happen?"

"Last year."

"Did you know who they were?"

"No," said the peasant, "but the knight... "

"Knight?" interrupted Leah, "a knight did this?"

"Yes m'lady."

"Did you recognise this knight?"

"No, but he did have a picture of a weasel on his shield."

"Huh! Sir Richard again."

Leah tosses a coin to the peasant who caught it.

"Thank you m'lady," the peasant smiles to expose his missing teeth again.

The two women prepare to leave the peasant and make their way to the church, but they notice a crowd has gathered around them. They express their gratitude at Leah returning.

"Welcome back m'lady"

"We can get this town back on its feet with you around again."

"Thank the Lord for your return."

Leah and Christine motioned their thanks, Holdfast shows his by barking and they all continue on their way.

Leah decides to pay a visit to the church; she goes to the nearest one which is Saint Mary's. She walks through the door whilst leaving Christine outside to look after the horses (and dog). Leah walks down the nave, her footsteps echo round the church. She hears something, not quite sure what so she stops and cocks her head to one side. It's like panting, like someone is out of breath, and then some moaning. Then all is quiet. Leah walks to the confession box and pulls back the curtain and Bishop Gilbert is there smoothing out his frock and a young lady, tying up her dress. Both turn their heads suddenly to the sound of the opening curtain.

"Hello, what's going here?" demands Leah.

"Oh, hello Lady Leah," says Bishop Gilbert.

The young woman runs past Leah and down the nave and exits the church.

"She was er... hum paying her tithe," says Gilbert.

"So I see."

"Have you come to confess?" asks the bishop.

"Yes, I have. What has become of the town?"

"Well, I did ask you to stop all this nonsense."

"Come now, are you saying that the demise of the town is my fault?"

"Well... "

"Because I'm a woman?"

"I don't make the rules, it comes from..." Bishop Gilbert points upwards.

"All I can do is ask for confession."

"All right go ahead."

Gilbert slaps his hand on Leah's head and pushes her down into a kneeling position.

"Our father in heaven... please forgive one your flock."

Leah exits the church.

"All fine my lady?"

"Indeed," says Leah, as she mounts her horse. "I am now without sin."

The two women ride on following the course of the River Lea, in the distance they can see Warden Hills standing proudly and majestically. Leah and Christine are nearly home when they come across a house.

"This wasn't here when we were last here," says Leah.

"Look," says Christine pointing, "it has a moat going all the way round it"

"It's not even a castle. It must be new."

"Yes, it's a moat house."

With that the intrepid pair carried on.

"I'm famished," said Christine.

"Always thinking of your stomach."

Near the end of their journey the Lea is but a small stream and they confront the castle. It is in a sorry state, the locals having robbed some of the walls of stone for their own buildings although much of the castle still stands.

"Aw, that looks sad," says Christine.

"We can get local builders to repair that. Remember, I'm now rich."

However they notice another building has been erected since they have been away. It stands on the other side of the Icknield Way to the castle.

"Look my lady, a new alehouse just across the road to your castle," says Christine.

"Oh yes. The Three Horseshoes, right next to my home too."

Their attention to the pub is shortlived as they ride through the entrance the large wooden doors broken off their hinges.

"Don't worry," says Christine. "I'll get onto those doors as soon as I can."

They dismount and there is no one around.

"Squire, bring my stuff in," says Leah, as she marches inside.

Christine lifts the battle gear off her weary horse and dumps it on the ground.

"First I must attend to the horses."

She leads them to the stables and fills up their pouches with fresh hay, then goes back to clear the mess off the floor.

Leah stands in her main hall and surveys the mess. The tapestry has been pulled down and trampled on. Her father's armour is no longer there, not a single bit of it, and all the weapons have been taken. She walks to the kitchen, cobwebs cover everything. There is no food anywhere but she does find a dusty bottle of wine. She opens it, sniffs it and takes a gulp.

"Yep, that's fine. Now I must attend to the garderobe."

Christine has gathered some wood together and totters into the main hall with her faithful hound following, she drops the wood on the floor causing Holdfast to jump back. She kneels by the wood and tosses a piece after piece into the grate; the dog's head follows each piece of wood. She puts some hay into the wood and prepares to light the fire, but she stops when Holdfast gives a stifled bark. Christine heard something too, not sure what it was but it was there. She turns her head suddenly and there, behind her are a man and a woman.

"Mister and missus Neville," she cries.

"Sorry to frighten you miss. We heard you were back," says Mister Neville.

"Never mind that. Put your things down and go and get some food."

Christine digs into her purse and gives the couple some coins.

"You know what me 'n' Leah like to eat."

"Yes my lady," say Mister Neville.

"Please, don't call me that. Just Christine will do."

With that, Mister Neville puts his hand to his head and both the couple turn towards the door.

"Oh, Mister and Mrs Neville," cries out Christine, stopping the pair in their tracks, "glad to have you back."

Mister and Mrs Neville say their thanks but Mrs Neville speaks up.

"Ahem... sorry to disturb you but I wondered... I mean we wondered... "

"Yes?" says Christine. "Out with it."

"It's just that Joan..." continued Mrs Neville.

"She used to work here," interrupts Mister Neville.

"Yes, she used to work, well I was wondering if she could erm..."

"Come back and work here?" asks Christine

The Nevilles turn to look at each other.

"All right, bring her back with you. She can help prepare the food."

The Nevilles mumble some thanks and quickly trot off to town.

Christine knows they will be several hours and so gets the fire going and heats up some water, she can hear Leah still in the garderobe straining. With the water boiled, she fills up a bath with rosemary leaves for her lady who has by now finished her business in the littlest room and quickly undresses to get in the bath.

"I will be clearing up for a while," Christine says to Leah who doesn't reply as she is too relaxed to care. Up goes the flag on the pole, the English flag of the red cross on a white background. Back downstairs Christine quickly sweeps the mess up from the floor with Holdfast running around the broom barking at it. She brushes the tapestry and hangs it back up, puts fresh hay on the floor, hangs up bunches of lavender and throws rose petals on the floor. And as the petals fall to the floor, Holdfast tries to catch them in his mouth. Christine has done her housework just as the Nevilles come back in with food. It is getting dark now and Mister and Mrs Neville start preparing the food in earnest while Leah settles down to the table in front of a roaring fire. The evening's meal has been prepared and Leah and her squire settle down to eat while the Neville's eat in the kitchen with Joan. Leah has her chicken prepared the English way while Christine has her beloved vegetable stew. Both have white bread, a luxury that only the well-off can afford.

It doesn't take long for whispers to pass through the grapevine and get to Sir Richard, who is in his mother's bedchamber.

"Richard darling" says Mother.

"Yes," replies Richard, who is never sure what his mother is up to.

"That lady knight, what's her name?"

"Leah."

"Er yes, Lady Leah. I've heard she's back in this country."

"So I've heard," says Richard, with agitation in his voice.

"Well, you know she could cause trouble for you."

"No, she can't do anything. People don't take women as knights very seriously."

"Nonetheless, I have heard that she has agreed to slay the dragon."

"So?"

Mother stands up and takes her son's hand.

"Don't you see, if she kills the dragon the people will love her."

"And your point is?"

Mother drops Richard's hand and turns away.

"You were never a bright boy, were you Richard?"

"What are you on about mother?"

Mother gracefully and slyly moves across the room and sits on the window seat staring out to the fields.

"What if you were to kill the dragon?" she eventually says after a quiet few minutes, much to the impatience of Richard.

"Hang about, that sounds dangerous."

Mother turns and stands up.

"Just think of it Richard darling. If you killed the dragon you would be a hero."

"Yes, but... "

"They will be talking about your heroic deeds all across this land."

"Yes," said Richard, looking upwards with his hands on his hips as if he is imagining something.

"They will be singing about you in sonnets for years to come."

A smile creeps across Richard's face.

"And they'll erect a statue of you in the town square with your foot on the defeated dragon's head."

Richard stands up straighter adding a couple of inches to his height.

"I like that," says an excited Richard.

"And the best thing about it..." Mother runs her finger down her son's chest.

"Yes," Richard says with both fists clenched in front of him.

"Lady Leah will be disgraced."

"Oh Mother, you are a genius."

With that Sir Richard runs out of the room.

Mother stood there and spoke to no one "I know."

"Christine," says Leah, with a goblet of wine in her hand, "can you build a cage?"

"Yes," says Christine. "How big?"

"About fifteen feet long by six feet by six feet. Yes, that should do it."

"You seem to know what this dragon is."

"So do you my dear, you came on the travels with me. Remember Egypt?"

"Oooh, one of them. I'll get on with the cage first thing in the morning."

Richard walks into his bedchamber where his wife is conversing with her ladies in waiting. Richard makes a motion with his face that his wife understands.

"Ladies." says Matilda to her waiting women. "Please leave us."

All the women depart from the room leaving only Richard and his wife.

"Richard," starts Matilda, "I have some news for you. I'm... "

"Lady Leah is back in this country," Richard interrupts, "and she intends to kill the dragon."

His wife just looks up at him.

"We can't have that," he mutters.

"You'll be ruined if she returns," she says. "You must stop her."

"I need to find this dragon first and slay it myself."

"I wouldn't go that far, that sounds dangerous. No, this lady knight must meet with..." Matilda pauses "... an unfortunate accident."

Sir Richard turns and walks with one hand on his chin and his other hand on his hip, he is deep in thought.

"Richard darling?" says Matilda. "Can we forget this affair and let me tell you... "

Richard turns and faces his wife to interrupt her again.

"No my dear, if I slay this dragon then not only will it disgrace this lady knight but it would make me look good."

No word from Matilda but Sir Richard continues:

"They will be talking about it for years to come, my name will be in sonnets and they'll erect a statue of me with my foot on the dragons head in the town square."

A trumpet sounds a fanfare outside the door.

"Hey!" shouts Richard towards the door, "don't be so sarcastic."

Chapter 7

The Preparation

It is the next morning and the king is in his chamber when his squire comes in.

"Sire," he says holding a silver tray on which sit two letters, "your majesty, letters for you."

"Thank you squire."

The squire walks out of the room while the king opens the first letter. He reads it.

"What does it say dear?" asks his wife

"It's from King Philippe; he says that he will never relinquish his crown."

He moves closer to his wife. "We will see my dear."

Meanwhile in France, Philippe is in court trying to relax but fidgets on his throne.

"I will never give up my crown to that English peeg. He is so... so... so... "

"Arrogant, your majesty?" says a nearby member of royal staff.

"Yes yes, arrogant. I like that... arrogant. I will scratch his eyes out. Ooh, it makes me sooooo mad thinking that an English king can lay claim to my throne. Just because his mother is French, he thinks he is too. Huh!"

His royal entourage continue staying in their exact positions and do not move. There is a painful few moments of silence. The king sits up suddenly and points.

"What is that?"

Everyone turns their heads towards the direction of the point.

"Mustard yellow with pink. They just do not go together. Ooh, get rid of the decorator, now!"

Philippe sits upright in a huff with his arms crossed.

King Edward has opened the second letter.

"Phillipa my dear, it seems we are invited to a meal at the castle of Sir Richard."

"And what is the occasion pray?"

"It seems that Sir Richard is so confident of capturing the dragon that he is hosting a celebratory meal."

"Ooh, I do love a party," squeals the queen. "I've never been to Sir Richard's castle."

"I think you will be disappointed with his abode," adds the king.

"When is the invitation for?" she asks.

"Two evening's time, he says the dragon's body will be on display."

"Ooh goody," says the queen "that will bring Lady Leah to shame."

Richard is being dressed in his armour by his squire. He also has now full plate armour but has taken the extra step of having black steel: a method of oxidising the metal by heating it to a very hot temperature (to just before melting) and then cooling very quickly in water. A process known as bluing and Richard was rich enough to afford it.

"Ballard, how well did you know Lady Leah?" Richard asks his squire.

"Very well," replies Ballard. "I watched her grow up"

Ballard places the breastplate up to Richard's chest and does up the fasteners.

"What are her weaknesses?"

"Well, she's a woman. She hasn't had any battle experience; I never saw her go to war."

"So she should be easy to subdue. What about her mother?"

"I never knew her, she left before I started working for Sir Bertram; he never talked about her."

"Hmm." Richard looked pensive. "Never mind, eh squire?"

"No Sire." Ballard bows low. "But it's when that Christine turned up. I should have been the one to look after the weapons but instead this woman from nowhere got that job."

Richard is no longer listening to his squire.

"When we have finished here let the staff know to prepare for tomorrow, we have royalty coming to dinner"

"Yes Sire."

Richard steps forward and raises his fist.

"I will be the greatest knight in this country."

"Yes, sire, I will follow you to the ends of the earth," says a bowed Ballard.

Preparations are also being made at Lygeton; Christine is busy getting equipment together while Leah is having breakfast on her own. Mrs Neville has brought in a plate of black pudding of which Leah's eyes light up with delight.

"You need to keep your strength up," says Mrs Neville as she places the plate on the table.

"Thank you, Mrs Neville," says Leah.

Leah is at ease about the whole business of capturing the dragon, capturing rather than slaying, as it would be more advantageous to keep the dragon alive. Leah is trying to imagine the look on people's faces when they encounter a real live dragon for the first time as she tucks into her black pudding. Leah looks around her castle; Christine has done a good job in restoring it back to its former glory, except for the empty corner where her father's armour should be. And where is the stuff that belonged to her mother? She's not sure if she can remember what she looked like and wonders where she is, now.

Leah has finished her breakfast and goes upstairs to get her stuff ready, but just has an inclination to look out of the window. Down in the courtyard Christine has reassembled the small forge, an open-air affair that has an overhanging covering. Christine pulls out a long piece of red molten metal which she transfers to the anvil. Christine herself is hot because today is unusually sunny and warm and she has her back exposed. Leah notices the muscles on the blacksmith's back and shoulders are well defined, and ripple in time with the movements of Christine's hammering. Slowly the piece of metal takes the shape of a sword; however Leah also notices the wooden cage next to the forge.

"Christine must have been up for hours," Leah thinks to herself.

Her attention is brought back to Christine when she hears the sound of steam erupting from the sword being dunked into a barrel of water. The sword is brought out and laid onto a bench where Christine has already made a handle previously; the handle is inserted onto the sword and hammered home. Leather is bound around the handle, the sword is complete. Leah is impressed with Christine's skill with materials.

Christine holds the sword up to admire, she is proud of her own work despite being told by the clergy that pride is evil. She swings the sword over her head and turns her body round on graceful steps. Leah thinks to herself that Christine learned all this just by watching her own skills. Christine swings the sword around and she thrusts it forward, the tip of the sword stopping inches from the face of Bishop Gilbert, who no one saw or heard come into the courtyard.

"Please don't hurt me!" pleads Bishop Gilbert, "it's only me."

Christine immediately retracts her sword.

"Please put all that flesh away," says Gilbert, still holding the reins of his small horse.

"This is a private residence," replies Christine as she puts on a jacket.

"Yes well, I've come to see Lady Leah."

"I am here, your grace," says Leah, walking out of the main building of her castle. "What can I do for you?"

"I've heard about this affair of you going after the dragon."

"My, word does get around quickly, doesn't it?"

"Look," says Gilbert, "I'm pleading with you to forget all this foolishness. It is foolhardy to chase after such an ungodly creature, let the real knights do it."

"I am a real knight." By now Leah was getting a bit agitated. "I've had battle experience."

"Yes but…" Gilbert could think of no other arguments to convince Leah to leave this venture alone.

"I'm… I mean we, are going after this dragon, with or without your approval. Now please, we have some preparation to do. We go to Bedford tomorrow."

Gilbert gives a slight bow and then mounts his horse. He trots out of the castle, but stops.

"I believe you have been invited to Sir Richard's meal, yes?" he says.

"No." replies Leah, "but I'm sure Sir Richard would want to see me there."

"What makes you say that?"

"Sir Richard will want to gloat," says Leah.

"Good, I may see tomorrow."

"You WILL see me tomorrow. I will defeat this dragon, just you see."

Gilbert eventually leaves the castle.

Leah turns her attention to the cage.

"How is this getting on?" she asks.

"It's nearly finished. I just have to bind the posts together with more strength; it will be ready before tomorrow."

Leah grabs a post and wiggles it.

"Seems sound enough," she says, "you have been up for hours now, how about something to eat?"

"I'll say," says Christine and the two women walk towards the castle door, but not before Leah picks up the newly made sword.

"I say," says Leah, swinging the sword around, "this is a finely balanced sword."

Richard is in the main hall of his castle describing his plans to his squire, with a few members of staff hanging around doing their normal everyday duties. Richard would normally tell his staff to go mind their own business but, today he is formulating the capture of the dragon so an audience is even better, especially when it comes to building up his own ego. Behind him is a large piece of parchment which has a picture of a dragon with a knight on a horse drawn on it (not very well at that).

"You will divert the dragon while I... "

"Me sire?"

"Yes you, squire. And don't interrupt me again. Now, as I was saying, you... squire... will keep the dragon's attention long enough for me to ride up and thrust my sword into its heart."

Richard stands with his hands on his hips looking very smug with himself, all the while hoping as many people as possible have heard what he has just said.

"What do you think... squire?" he leans forward close to his squire and says in a lower volume, "sorry, I can't remember your name."

"Ballard sire."

"Yes... Ballard. What do you think of my plan, Ballard my good man?"

"Brilliant sire," says Ballard, with excitement in his voice but his face betrays his true feelings which are opposite to his speech. "A good plan."

"And you are with me," with this Richard emphasises his squire's name, "Ballard?"

"Oh yes sire." says Ballard. "I'm with you all the way, sire."

"Good, go prepare my horse... erm" Richard tries desperately to remember his squire's name, "... Ballard."

"Yes sire, straight away." Ballard runs out of the room leaving Richard standing as tall as he can stretch himself in front of the picture of the badly drawn dragon and knight hoping all the staff have seen this memorable scene.

"Richard darling!" comes a call from the other side of the main hall, "I have some news for you."

"Not now my dear. I'm going to be the greatest knight in the entire world."

He tries to stand even taller but then has an idea. He draws his sword and holds it aloft.

"I'm going to kill this dragon."

This time the staff does look around at Richard, making him feel even more important.

"It's a letter for my lady," says Christine.

"Open it," Leah replies looking at the newly made sword.

Christine breaks the seal and opens up the letter; Holdfast is sitting at the feet of his mistress.

"Read it to me," Leah says again not taking her eyes off the sword.

"It's an invitation."

Leah stops turning the sword around and turns towards her squire.

"An invitation to where?"

"Sir Richard has invited you to dinner."

"When?"

"Tomorrow night." Christine drops her arms and moves forward as if to emphasise a point. "And get this."

She pulls the invitation back up to read whilst stepping back, much to the discomfort of Holdfast who was comfortable sitting next to Christine's legs.

"It's a dragon-slaying celebration. Listen to this, 'the body of the dragon will be on display'. Can you believe that?"

Leah stands up. "Yes I can, I knew he would send an invitation. I told you, he wants to gloat."

She holds the new sword aloft.

"Tomorrow we go to bed," declares Lady Leah, "but first to Bedford."

Christine tries to correct Leah. "I think you mean first to bed and then to Bedford."

"Yes, that's what I said."

Chapter 8

The Dragon

Living in Bedford, Sir Richard has an advantage over Leah as he is closer to the site where the dragon was reported to have been seen, which is near Caudwell Priory near the Great River Ouse. Next to the river is a lake which is where the reports of the dragon seem to point to; Richard is on his horse whilst Ballard is walking behind carrying the armour. He is out of breath and sweating profusely, but he has to keep up or risk losing his job.

"How many people have died from this dragon, squire?" asks Richard.

"Five, I think," Ballard pants.

"I heard it was six... or even seven. Still, the hero has turned up to vanquish this foul beast."

"Yes sire"

"Hold it." Richard stops his horse.

"What is it, sire?"

"Over there, there's something just past those trees." Richard points. "Looks like it's waiting in a cave."

Leah and Christine arrive much later south of Bedford; the priory can be seen off in the distance. A wooden cage on two wheels is attached to Christine's horse.

"We've tracked it thus far, the monster must be close by," says Leah. "Bring the cage through this clearing. I believe there is a lake nearby."

They continue through the clearing with the cage creaking as it moves along. They find an old man sitting by the entrance of a small cave.

"Old man," demands Leah, "we have heard there is a dragon here."

"He took my dinner," said the man rather pathetically.

"We are interested in the dragon," reiterates Leah.

"It was a nice umble stew and he took it."

"Who took your umble stew?"

"A knight. He had a weasel on his shield."

Leah and Christine look at each other and say in unison, "Sir Richard."

Leah then turns her attention back to the old man.

"We'll deal with him later but first we want to know where this dragon is."

The man points and says, "Over there."

"Thank you old man," says Leah, and throws a coin at the man's feet before riding off.

"My name is Antwon the monk!" shouts the old man after the pair.

"What's umble stew?" asks Leah.

"It's a stew..." replies Christine, "made from heart, liver and testicles of a deer."

"Yuk! That doesn't sound very nice."

"It's the horrible bits that no one else wants. Umble stew is what the peasants eat."

"Oh," says Leah, with something going through her mind.

Leah and Christine reach a clearing in the woods, Holdfast is barking towards a clump of trees.

"I think, my Lady that he is here," says Christine.

They both stop their horses and dismount; Christine quickly unhooks the cage and wheels it into place. Suddenly Holdfast starts barking at the water's edge.

"You don't have to tell me squire. Holdfast knows the dragon is there." says Leah

Suddenly Sir Richard steps out from the trees in his black armour, closely followed by his squire Ballard.

"Not so fast," he says waving his sword around.

"What is the meaning of this?" demands Leah. "Ballard? I see you've switched sides."

"You'll not slay this dragon," says Richard.

"Yea, methinks so."

"Nay, methinks not, I want that glory," says Richard but he is totally unaware of the dark shape gliding through the water behind him.

"We can't have a woman knight taking all the glory," says Richard. "I mean, what would become of the world if women were doing men's jobs?"

"A better place," replies Leah.

"Don't be so facetious," says an angry Richard.

The dark shape glides closer to Richard's feet that are close by the edge of the lake; the lumps that cover the dragon's back are clearly visible and its eyes above the water whilst the rest of its head is unseen below.

"I don't want to worry you," says Leah, "but I think the dragon is behind you."

"You can't fool me, I'm a man and I'm not so easily fooled."

"Yes well, it's right behind you."

Richard turns his head slightly while still looking at Leah and Christine. He gives quick glance then turns back.

"See? Nothing there."

Ballard speaks up now.

"My Lord, I think she's right."

"Don't be so stupid, squire," says Richard angrily.

But to no avail, Ballard drops Richard's weapons and makes a run for it.

"It's the dragon!" he cries, as he runs off.

"Come back you coward!" shouts Richard.

With everyone's attention diverted to the fleeing squire, the dragon thrusts itself out of the water, grabs Sir Richard by the calves and pulls him into the water. Holdfast bolts into the safety of the woods. The dragon then executes a death roll, turning the knight over and over, with his armour making a clanging sound on each turn. Sir Richard declares his pain.

"Ow! Ow! Ow!" he goes each time he is turned over.

"Christine, the rope," says a calm Leah with an outstretched arm.

Her squire gets the rope off the back of her horse and hands it to Leah, who then ties the end of the rope into a noose. She steps over to the edge of the lake and the dragon stops, releasing Sir Richard who then crawls away. The dragon looks into Lady Leah's eyes and then pounces. But Leah is ready and steps to the side with the noose hanging in front of the dragon. The creature thrusts its snout through the loop of rope and Leah pulls, tightening the dragon's long mouth shut. She then sits on top of the scaly reptile, pulls its head right back with the noose and winds the rope around the snout of the dragon.

Leah steps off the creature while it thrashes about a bit. Meanwhile, Sir Richard has regathered his composure and picks up his sword. As he stands there with his sword held up, water pours out of various openings in Richard's armour. Everyone stops to watch until, finally water stops pouring out.

"Now m'lady. It's time to dispense with you," says Sir Richard.

Leah withdraws her sword slowly (the one Christine made the day before) and holds it with both hands in front of her. Christine covers her mouth with her hands. Holdfast pokes his head out from some ferns, whimpers, then quickly retracts his head back into the ferns.

"You beat me last time," says Richard, "but not this time. I will defeat you easily."

"Have you had battle experience?" asks Leah.

"Yes," replies Richard.

"What battle?"

"Er... the battle of..." a pause "... Bedford."

"Hah! No such battle. You haven't actually fought in warfare have you?"

This last comment enrages Richard and he swings his sword over his head, yet Leah parries the blow. She then tries a side swipe but Richard blocks her blow. The dragon's eyes follow the movements of the two knights who both step back from each other.

"I've been meaning to ask you, Sir Richard."

"What?" replies Richard as he swings his sword towards Leah's chest, but she blocks the attack easily.

"If you have no battle experience then how comes you are so rich?"

"CLANG." Another blocked strike from Richard.

"That's easy to answer. What I do now."

"What are you doing now?" demands Leah.

"I discredit knights and they pay me to keep my mouth shut."

Richard takes another over-arm swipe but Leah steps to one side and Richard's sword misses its target. Richard is slightly off balance and Leah boots him in the backside. He regains his balance and turns.

"Just as I'm going to discredit you. The glory of capturing the dragon will go to me and you will be exiled again."

Three swipes from Richard all of which are blocked by Leah, the last block being a twirling movement which flicks the sword out of Richard's hands. The sword flies through the air and thrusts into the soil in front of Christine, who with both hands grabs the sword and holds it up.

"My squire is just as good with the sword as I am," says Leah, holding her own sword to Richard's face. "Who do you think I train with?"

Sir Richard stands still with his hands held up.

"Now Sir Richard, you are in an uncompromising position, are you not?"

"You'll never get away with this!" wails Sir Richard.

"Oh but I have, and what's more we have had an audience."

"What? Who? Where?" stammered Richard unable to think of anything sensible to say.

"The old man whose dinner you stole."

"I was hungry."

"It was umble stew, a peasant's food. How do you think people would view that?"

"I can get round that one."

"Yes well, I don't know exactly where he is but I do know he is watching."

"Yeah, so?"

"Well, can you imagine how people will react when they find out you were defeated in battle by a woman."

"Oh God, no. Not again!" weeps Richard.

"Now I won't tell anyone," Leah looks up and says very loudly, "and I'm sure no one else will either."

Richard falls to his knees. "What's the deal?"

"Give the old man a home, food and clothing."

"What, you mean that miserable, old...?"

"Oh well," interrupts Leah while turning away from Richard and shouts, "you might as well tell everyone."

"No!" Richard raises a hand to nowhere in particular, not knowing where the old man is.

"Good, that's settled then, I'll let you go and you can welcome the old man into your castle tonight for a hearty meal, yes?"

Christine throws the sword to the ground in front of Richard.

"What will I tell my wife?" Richard asks as he stands up

"Hmm, that's your problem. Now go."

Richard scrambles off with his sword but is stopped by Leah calling out:

"Perhaps also you could make a monthly charitable donation to the town of Lygeton."

"What? That's unfair!" wails Sir Richard.

"Well, it was you who destroyed the town."

"Yes all right," and Richard shuffles off.

The whole time the dragon has been lying still in the water, just watching with its mouth trussed up.

"Christine, open the cage."

Christine pulls open the door while Leah prods the dragon with her sword. The dragon responds by running into the cage, Holdfast runs out of the ferns and jumps onto the monster's back, which is fifteen feet long including the tail which took up nearly half the length of its body.

"Get out of there," demands Christine.

Holdfast jumps off and trots out of the cage, enabling Christine to close it up. Holdfast barks at the dragon, but the dragon just looks at the dog with its green eyes that have just a vertical slit for the pupil. Holdfast doesn't like the dragon and runs off.

"Scaredy cat!" shouts Christine after the dog as she closes the cage up.

Leah puts her sword away in its sheath.

"That should make a fine sideshow for someone," says Leah, with her hands on her hips.

Richard is on his horse making his sad way back home, unable to think of any excuses as to why he didn't kill the dragon. As he slowly trots through the woods he finds Ballard sitting in a small space between a tree's roots, weeping and rocking back and forth.

"That dragon breathed fire," he said

"Ballard."

"And had wings."

Richard says, "What? No it didn't have any of that."

"It was the biggest thing I'd ever seen."

"BALLARD!"

The weeping man stops rocking.

"You're fired Ballard," says Richard. "You can stay here for the rest of your days if you like, for all I care."

With that Richard carries on, leaving Ballard to continue rocking back and forth.

Leah and Christine have travelled from Bedford to Lygeton with the dragon in the cage strapped to Christine's horse. As they near the town on the Bedford Road crowds rush to the pair and gather around the cage, they stare and gawp at the captured creature.

"It's a dragon!" they cry.

Children jump up and down with joy, adults gasp in amazement while the cage slowly creaks on and the people follow it. In the centre of Lygeton Leah stops.

"People of Lygeton!" she cries out. "Behold the dragon!"

The crowd cheers.

"I bequeath this dragon to the town of Lygeton. You must house it and feed it; people will come from miles around to pay to see this creature. You will soon have enough money to rebuild the town of Lygeton."

More roars from the crowd and people dance with joy. Leah looks at Christine.

"This will be one in the eye for Sir Richard."

"Indeed my lady."

Leah raises her hands to silence the crowd. She addresses them again:

"We will take the dragon away to show the king this evening, but I promise I will bring it back again tomorrow when you will start building the enclosure. Long live the king."

The crowd roar with excitement again. Leah and Christine are about to start back to the castle when a little girl comes up to them. She raises her hand which is holding a rose. Leah bends down to pick the flower from the girl, the little girl stretching as far as she can stretch to hand over the rose.

"Thank you," says Leah who tucks the rose into a crevice on her breastplate.

The little girl speaks, "I want to be a knight just like you."

The crowd laugh but Leah holds up a hand and the crowd go silent. She leans over and speaks to the girl.

"What be your name, little girl?"

"Ethelfleda," comes the reply.

"A fine Saxon name," says Leah. "Never let go of your dreams."

The pair of women work their way round and through the crowd on their way back to their castle. The crowd roar with excitement as the cage creaks past them and the dragon thrashes about a bit. People poke their hands through the bars of the cage to touch the dragon, knowing it won't bite them due to its mouth being trussed up. Leah turns on her horse and waves at the little girl.

Back at her castle Leah is getting ready when there is a knock on her door.

"Yes?" she asks.

In steps Mrs Neville.

"Ahem my lady, there's a gentleman downstairs saying 'e 'as a gift."

"Alright, I'll be right down."

Leah looks at herself in the mirror at her fine pink dress and then walks out of the room. Downstairs Christine is already there.

"There's some chap here with a gift for you," she says.

"Come now man," says Leah to the young man, "what is it?"

"Are you Lady Leah?" he asks nervously.

"I am," she replies.

He pulls out from his pouch an object wrapped in linen.

"It's a gift from a Madame Gus... Gust-vee... "

"Gaste-Viande?" says Christine.

"That's it, yes. She sent me with this gift for you."

Leah takes the object and unwinds the linen, inside is a bottle of wine.

"It's some wine from Gaste-Viande's vineyard. What a wonderful present," says Leah.

She hands a coin to the boy and dismisses him.

"We must write to her and let her know everything is all right here," says Christine.

"And tell her about the dragon."

Leah looks at the handwritten label on the bottle.

"We can take this to the dinner tonight, shan't we squire?"

"Yes, m'lady."

Chapter 9

The Meal

Sir Richard is hosting a meal for the king and queen. The table spreads out like a horseshoe with the royals, Sir Richard and his wife at the head. Down one side to Richard's right are the apprentice knights from the joust five years ago who are no longer apprentices but fully fledged knights and dressed in full armour now, looking resplendent. To Richard's left are the other guests including Richard's mother, Bishop Gilbert, Lord Zuckerman, Christine, Lady Leah and Antwon the mad monk. Except that the places where Leah and Christine should be there is no Leah and Christine.

There is a whole array of food from Richard's estate, mostly fowl and fish, with vegetables and white bread.

"Your majesty, there is some French food here," says Richard to the king.

"I don't want that rubbish. Too much garlic, take it away," replies the king.

"I say Sir Richard," continues the king. "I thought you had invited Lady Leah and her squire. They don't seem to be here."

"I did," Richard replied, "but they seem to be late."

Richard mumbles under his breathe, "I hope they don't show up at all."

Behind the head of the table on the wall is the family tapestry showing the sign of the weasel. Richard looks glum; Matilda leans over and asks, "Why did you have to bring that old man in."

The old man in question is the old man by the lake.

"I'll have a piece of that chicken, a roast joint and some of that sweetmeat over there," says Antwon.

The serving wench replies, "You can have a piece of that chicken, a roast joint but you can't have that sweetmeat over there."

The old man reiterates his request. "I'll have a piece of that chicken, a roast joint and some of that sweetmeat over there."

The serving wench replies again, "I said, you can have a piece of that chicken, a roast joint but you can't have that sweetmeat over there."

And so on.

Sir Richard replies to his wife's earlier question, "It's a favour for a friend."

The king leans over from the other side of Richard. "Here, did you find that old man?"

Sir Richard just sighs.

Just then, Lady Leah walks in her long pale pink shimmering dress.

"Ah," says the king. "You have arrived."

Richard slumps further into his chair.

"Good eventide, your majesty," replies Leah.

"Pray, what is your excuse for such lateness?" asks the king.

Richard sits up a little with a hope that Leah would be in trouble.

"Your majesty, may I present to you the dragon?" Leah holds out an outstretched hand.

"You slew it then and not Richard?"

"Your majesty," Leah remarks, "slay the dragon? I think not."

She holds her hand out again towards the door.

"Your majesty. Gentles and ladies. Sires and squires. May I present to you, the dragon."

A creaking sound is heard followed by Christine in her long green dress; she is holding two wooden poles. Attached to the poles is the cage which is wheeled in by Christine's strength. In the cage is the dragon to which the people show gasps of amazement. The dragon thrashes a bit, causing the guests to be slightly disconcerted, then the creature settles down.

"My word!" exclaims the king. "It truly is a dragon."

"And this," Leah places a bottle in front of the king.

"What's this?" asks the king.

"Wine from Languedoc."

"Ooh, I say," says the king.

Leah and Christine take their places, not that anyone has noticed because the dragon is now their fascination. Also not noticed is a whitish bundle of fur travelling quickly across the floor and zipping under the table.

The entertainment is a man with a dancing bear. Bears are common in Europe and many people try to scrape together a living by importing young bears and teaching them tricks. However, despite Sir Richard being rich, he scrimps on entertainment and also is not a good judge of what is entertaining. The bear shuffles uneasily on its hind feet and waves its front paws around. Behind him his owner pulls the chain that holds the bear, the man holds a pointed stick and the bear looks worried, but no one really notices as the dragon is far more interesting.

"What is this rubbish?" demands the queen.

"Sir Richard." The king turns to face the knight. "Get rid of this... excuse for a good time."

Sir Richard claps his hands and two serfs grab the man by his arms and pull him away. The bear also follows as his chain has been tugged.

"Please sir," wails the man, "at least some food, the bear is very hungry you know."

"You're fired," says Lord Zuckerman.

Both the bear and its owner are thrown out of the castle

Lady Leah and Christine are tucking into their food; they glance at the dragon in the cage.

"Well, squire, I should have my pardon now although the king won't let me fight in this war. Never mind, we can't have everything."

Christine doesn't reply as she has a mouthful of vegetable stew.

"I have to say this is a warm castle," says Leah.

Leah looks up to the windows which have inserted into them stained glass panes in lead. Leah turns to Sir Richard.

"Sir Richard," she asks, "how do you keep the castle so warm?"

"It's the glass windows," Richard replies, while motioning towards the said windows with his eyes, "it's the latest castle accessory you know."

Leah also notices the suit of armour in the corner of the room which happens to look like her father's armour.

"I say, that is a fine suit of armour over there, looks just like my father's."

"Only the best is what I buy," replies Richard.

"Tell me Sir Richard," continues Leah, "how do you afford all these riches?"

Richard looks uncomfortable and squirms in his seat

"If you like the suit of armour I will present it to you as a gift."

Leah nods her head but quickly notices Christine tearing off some pieces of chicken and placing them under the table.

"Christine, you haven't turned meat eater have you?" asks Leah.

"No," replies Christine and she pulls the table cloth back a bit to reveal Holdfast's head, happily chewing the chicken pieces. Leah smiles and pats the dog's head.

"I think we can keep him," says Leah.

Christine smiles.

The king shouts over to Leah, "Fine job you did of capturing the dragon."

The dragon is in its cage sitting quietly until someone throws a piece of meat. This the dragon catches it in its open mouth, showing rows of pointed teeth.

"Thank you your highness. It's a crocodrillus."

"A what?" he asks

"A crocodrillus, I saw lots of them in North Africa."

The king looks perplexed.

"You mean to say there are more of those things out there?"

"Your majesty," asks Lady Leah, "are you sure you wouldn't want me to go to this war with France with you?"

"No sorry, we don't have women in the army. However, Sir Richard... "

Richard turns to face the king who continues:

"... I would expect you to join me in this war."

"Yes, your majesty," says Richard who then turns in the other direction.

"Mother!" he calls.

"What, my dear?" she replies.

"The King wants me to go to war with him."

"And so you should, make a man of you."

"But mother, I don't want to go. What do I do?"

"Don't ask me, just go."

Richard slumps in his chair whilst Mother leans forward to grab some of that delicious sweetmeat. Leah happens to be also glancing at the sweetmeat when she notices Richard's mother. She had never seen Richard's parents but this woman looks familiar. Leah leans forward to see around Bishop

Gilbert and Christine. She can't quite see so she stands up and looks.

"What are you looking at?" asks Richard.

"Mother?" asks Leah.

Mother looks up, then the sudden realisation on her face.

"Yes, it is you Mother."

Richard suddenly becomes aware of what is going on.

"She's your mother?" he asks.

"Yes, she left me when I was quite young, but..." she turns her face towards Mother, "I still remember her."

Leah sits down again. Richard is almost in tears.

"Is this true Mother?" he asks of his mother.

"Well..." she stammers "... I did have a daughter years ago with a knight."

"Which knight?" asks Leah.

Mother turns to Richard and says to her son, "Your father was Sir Bertram. I left after a disagreement... er more like an argument and I set up in a castle under your name, Richard."

"So I didn't inherit the castle like you said?"

"No, it was with Sir Bertram's money. He helped us; he never forgave me but we never divorced."

"So you didn't run off with another man then?" asks Leah.

"No, we were still married. Your father wouldn't change his will and I wanted Richard to have the castle, not you, but he was adamant that you Leah had everything."

"You know what this means then?" wails Richard.

"What does it mean?" says Leah and mother in unison.

"Lady Leah is my elder sister," he moans.

"Har-har!" laughs Christine.

Leah continues eating but Richard and his mother sit and look glum and don't talk or even exchange glances. Matilda, who up to now has been quiet, suddenly says something.

"I have some news."

"No news right now would be welcomed," says a glum Richard.

"I'm going to have a baby," says Matilda.

A smile creeps across Richard's face.

"That is good news. Why didn't you tell me before, my dear?"

"I tried to, but you were so busy with this dragon business."

"I'm going to have a niece," says an overjoyed Leah.

"I hope not, it's got to be a boy," says Richard.

For the first time Richard and Leah laugh together.

Now a jester prances in front of the eating guests; he juggles but the balls just fall all over the floor. He hits himself over the head with a leather balloon tied to the end of a stick.

"A horse walks into an alehouse and the barman asks, why the long face?"

No one is laughing at the jester's jokes.

"Boo!" the guests show their disappreciation.

Two serfs grab the jester by the arms and drag him off.

"No no, not yet. Tell me if you've heard this one? There was an Irishman, a Scotsman and an Englishman... "

The rest of the joke will never be told at this dinner as the jester is thrown out of the castle. The door slams behind him and he bangs on it.

"Let me in, I can be funny."

The jester hears a growl and slowly turns his head. His face is close to a snarling bear's face and on the end of its chain is his owner.

"He's a hungry bear you know," says the owner.

The jester drops his stick with the bells on the end and they jingle as they hit the floor. The bear licks its lips.

Musicians replace the jester and they play their instruments. Most of the meal has been finished and the servants are bringing round oranges. The king picks one up and sinks his teeth into it and promptly spits out his mouthful.

"No your majesty, it's an orange and you peel it first," says Sir Richard while he demonstrates.

The king watches in fascination and then proceeds to peel his own. He bites into the sweet fruit.

"Mmm! It's really nice," says the king. "Try one my dear," he adds as he hands an orange to his wife.

"They've just recently been brought into this country," Richard boasts.

"Christine," says Leah to her squire, "I have decided that we will go travelling again."

"Oh? Where to?" asks a suspicious-looking Christine.

"Oh, I don't know, maybe the Far East."

"Won't south of France do? I like it there and we can visit Madame Gaste-Viande again."

"Not really, we're at war with France, remember?"

Leah thinks a moment.

"I know; we could go to Germany. I've heard women have more rights there."

Bishop Gilbert overhears the conversation and tells Lady Leah, "I'm going on a pilgrimage next week before this war hots up too much."

"Where are you going?"

"To see the Pope."

"Oh you're going to Rome?"

"No, the Pope resides at Avignon."

"Where's that?"

"In the south of France."

Gilbert takes another swig of ale from his flagon while Leah turns to Christine. "Have we been to Avignon?"

"Yes, we saw the Pope there."

"What? When did he move there? And why did no one tell me?"

"I did," mumbled Christine, "lots of times."

The king overheard the conversation "so, you've seen the Pope then?"

"Yes." says Christine.

"Did he talk about me at all?" asked the king.

"He did say that he favoured you over Philippe."

"Did he now? But he's French, isn't he?"

"I believe the pair of them do not get on your majesty."

The king replies to Leah. "I say, your squire is very knowledgeable, Lady Leah."

"Yes your majesty, she an eternal fountain of knowledge."

The king settles back in his chair with a satisfied look on his face.

Bishop Gilbert has been quaffing ale all evening and is a bit merry, he continues eating a chicken leg and has made a mess of his fingers; he holds them up not knowing where to wipe them. A wench brings a napkin over.

"Thank you my dear," says Gilbert taking the napkin he wipes his fingers. "You're very kind, food can be so messy."

"You're welcome, your bishopness."

"But I must say I do love chicken with my ale. Cheers!" he raises his flagon of ale to the wench. "I say my dear, have you paid your tithe lately?"

The King's squire calls out loudly, "Quiet please!"

The noise slowly dies down; the squire speaks again. "His majesty would like to speak."

The king stands up.

"Ladies and gentlemen, my honourable knights," he begins, flourishing an arm at their expectant faces.

"We are presently at a state of war with France."

A few murmurs here and there

"And we will meet them on their own ground. Soon we will sail across the Channel and march from Calais. I expect every knight here to do his duty for their King."

All the knights cheer and raise their goblets towards the king, although Sir Richard doesn't put much energy into his actions.

"Good, for the glory of England then."

All raise their goblets and cry out, "Long live the king!"

Still standing the king calls out to Leah.

"Lady Leah, I understand you play the lute? Come on, get up and play for us."

Leah gets up while the king sits down. She picks up a lute and, with Christine on the tambourine, they start playing for the small party who thoroughly enjoy the music. Leah sings a sonnet she had written:

> *For thou'st do nothing but dream*
> *For thou'st would not follow your desire*
> *One must follow your thought-up scheme*
> *For your dream won't achieve higher*
> *Shackled by these rusty irons*
> *Free one's self by thine own hand*
> *Work for those three golden lions*
> *For love no greater than England*
> *But forget not your dream thou hast followed*
> *And pursue within reason your goal*
> *Remove self-pity that you wallowed*
> *Mayhap you soon see yourself whole*